THE NOCTURNALS

Book Four
The Hidden Kingdom

Tracey Hecht and Sarah Fieber

Fabled Films Press
New York

Published by Fabled Films LLC, New York

ISBN: 978-1-944020-11-8

Library of Congress Control Number: 2017951811

First Edition: February 2018

1 3 5 7 9 10 8 6 4 2

Cover Designed by Jaime Mendola-Hobbie
Interior Book Design by Notion Studio
Typeset in Stemple Garamond, Mrs. Ant and Pacific Northwest
Printed by Everbest in China

FABLED FILMS PRESS
NEW YORK CITY
www.fabledfilms.com

For information on bulk purchases for promotional use please contact Consortium Book Sales & Distribution at ingrampublishersvcs@ingramcontent.com or 1-866-400-5351

To the Hidden Kingdom of Fabled Films Press,
Stacey, Nicole, Gisselle, Lisette, Jerry
You make our magic happen!

Book Four
The Hidden Kingdom

Chapter One
THE PARCHED PANGOLIN

"Oh goodness." Tobin yawned and gazed up at the evening sky. The stars and moon were shining—it was time for his nightly adventure. But after a day of tossing and turning in the scratchy leaves of his burrow, the pangolin awoke tired, hungry, and thirsty. It was the valley's dry season. There was little to eat or drink. And Tobin, known for eating a bit more food than most, was having an especially difficult time. Tonight, his throat was parched, his belly grumbled...and adventure was the furthest thing from his mind.

The pangolin stretched his anteater-like body. His eyes felt scratchy in the dry night air, and his leaf-like scales were cracked and creased, like the skin of a crocodile.

Tobin sighed then set off in search of even the tiniest snack or sip. He slowly trudged toward the bushes, sniffing the ground with his sensitive snout.

Usually, he could smell all kinds of things—the dew-covered petals of daffodils, the tangy rinds of oranges, the musky bark of big oaks. But recently, he could smell only dry earth and brown grass, scorched to death by the heat.

Except…wait a moment. Tobin's snout suddenly perked up. "Could it be?" Somehow, he had picked up a trace of moisture—the scent, he believed, of damp rock. Tobin's pace quickened into an eager trot. His mind danced with visions of flowing water, lush moss, and juicy termites.

He traveled just a short distance, but he was breathless when he reached his destination—a narrow opening in a wall of rock. The pangolin grinned—he had been right. There was water here. It wasn't exactly flowing from the crack. Actually, it was barely trickling. But it was water nonetheless.

Tobin closed his eyes and uncurled his long tongue—so long, in fact, that he kept it coiled inside his stomach when he wasn't using it. But now, he stretched it to its full, remarkable length, eager to catch the next drop.

"Hey! *Pangolino*!" Before even a single, cool drip could land on Tobin's parched tongue, he heard a loud, shrill voice calling to him from above.

Tobin gazed up. Perched high on a tree branch was his friend Bismark, a sugar glider—a tiny marsupial similar to a flying squirrel. Like Tobin, Bismark was nocturnal: awake by night, asleep by day. And, like Tobin, Bismark was hungry and thirsty.

The sugar glider spread his flaps—the stretchy skin that connected his arms and legs. Then, with a graceful leap, he glided down from his tree and joined his friend on the ground. "Have you seen what the drought has done to my poor pomelos?" he asked. Bismark opened his paws, revealing a lumpy fruit with a dark, shriveled rind.

Tobin shook his head. This was very upsetting. The grapefruit-like pomelos that grew on his friend's tree were usually plump and juicy.

"And it's not just my favorite fruit that has withered," moaned Bismark. "Look at me! Never has my soft, gray fur been so drab, so dreary, so dry." With an impatient shove, the sugar glider pushed Tobin aside. "Out of the way, *pangolino!*" he ordered, jumping in front of the crack in the rock. "I need water, too!" Then he closed his eyes, opened his mouth, and tilted back his head. As a droplet of water fell onto his tongue, Bismark shuddered in delight. He spread his legs wide and dug his tiny heels in the ground, positioning himself for the next spurt of water. But alas—no more came. The trickle had come to an abrupt halt.

"What? *Qué? Quoi?*" The sugar glider pounded his fist on the stone, urging the water to flow. But all that seeped from the crack was a fine mist of dust that settled on his nose and prompted a sharp, high-pitched sneeze.

"This is unacceptable, unsatisfactable, un-stinking-fair!" Bismark sputtered, stomping his feet in outrage. He turned to Tobin. "You think that one little droplet is enough for this breathtaking body...this fabulous physique?" The sugar glider flexed his small muscles. Then, he spun on his toes in a circle, attempting to show himself off.

"Um...." Tobin's voice trailed. There was no use in telling Bismark that, judging by size alone, he didn't need that much water.

"Really, *compadre*, in the name of the night," Bismark continued, "why did you steal all the water from your best and most brilliant *amigo*, hmm?"

"Oh goodness...I...I didn't even have one—" Tobin stopped when he heard soft footsteps nearby. He knew the sound of those paws. The pangolin turned toward the brush. Sure enough, a fox emerged with a quiet rustle. It was his friend Dawn.

Immediately, Bismark scampered alongside the

fox. "My bella Dawn, my sweet, *mon amour*—you've awakened! And, behold: my thirst has been quenched after all. Your radiant, red fur can brighten even the driest and darkest of evenings!"

Tobin smiled. Dawn was the leader of the Nocturnal Brigade—the group the three friends had formed to rescue animals in need of their help. And Bismark was right—she could bring comfort and light, even in the most difficult times. But the sugar glider's not-so-secret love for the fox was affecting his vision—though Dawn always looked poised and polished, her fur was more dull than radiant at the moment. Even the strongest animals of the valley, like the fox, were hurt by the drought. Especially droughts as severe as this one.

Dawn cleared her throat with a raspy cough.

"Oh, *mon amour*! You sound totally parched. You know…" Bismark mused, stroking the fur on his chin, "I managed to find a little sip of water just before you arrived. It's gone now," he continued, shooting Tobin a glare. "But I think there miiiiight still be a little moisture left on my lips…." The sugar glider gazed up at Dawn. He batted the lids over his dark, bulbous eyes. Then he stood as tall as he could on his tiptoes and pressed his lips into a pucker.

But the fox barely noticed her friend's antics. Her

amber eyes were fixed on something in the distance. "Do you see that?" she asked. She pointed to some roundish objects.

Tobin squinted, trying to see what they were, but his eyesight was poor. "Oh goodness," he said with a sigh. "I see something out there. But it all just looks fuzzy to me."

"Exactly," said Dawn. A gust of wind began to blow. As its speed picked up, the fuzzy spots Tobin had seen moved closer. At once, Dawn bolted toward them. "I'll be right back," she called over her shoulder.

"What is she doing?" asked Tobin. "What's that she's running to?"

"I hate to admit it, *amigo*," said Bismark, "but I don't know. It appears that this despicable dryness has taken its toll on the sheen of my coat *and* on my eyesight! It's all a blur, I tell you. A fuzzy blur!" He craned his neck. "Though my lovely Dawn remains clear as ever."

Starry-eyed, Bismark kept his gaze fixed on the fox until she returned with a tan, hay-like ball about the size of a large pumpkin. With her snout, the fox gently nudged it toward her two friends.

Tobin smiled. His eyes hadn't failed him after all! It was fuzz—or a tumbleweed to be more precise. He should have known: tangles of it entered the valley each dry season. He sniffed it just to be sure. "Tumbleweed," he confirmed. "It looks strange, though."

"Yes," agreed Dawn. "I was thinking the same thing this evening when I first saw it. It's unlike any tumbleweed we've seen before." The fox circled the grassy ball. "Its seeds and sticks appear different."

"*Blech!*" Bismark sputtered. "I detest tumbleweeds—the old kind and the new!" The sugar glider glowered at the odd, fuzzy ball. "Prepare to fight, you messy menace, you sticky stranger, you ugly orb!"

With that, Bismark reeled back his leg and punted the tumbleweed with a mighty kick, sending it bouncing into the clearing.

Eeeeee!

Suddenly, a shrill shriek pierced the air. The trio looked at one another in alarm.

"Was that you, my parched *pangolino*?" asked Bismark. "You *have* been known to emit strange sounds...but I haven't heard *that* one before."

"Oh goodness, no," replied Tobin. The pangolin blushed. He did have an active rear, tooting from time to time and letting out a potent, defensive odor when he got scared. But this time, Tobin had not done a thing. "It really wasn't me," he said.

"Then what was it?" asked Bismark.

The sugar glider and the pangolin turned to Dawn. She always seemed to know the answer to unusual questions like this. But even the fox looked confused. She took a step forward and studied the land. Then, with pricked ears and a craned neck, she listened more closely.

The scream-like sound came right from the clearing—not far from where they stood. But there was no trace of anyone there. So where, they all wondered, had it come from?

Chapter Two
HELP!

"Yoo-hoo!" called Bismark, cupping his hands to his mouth. "Who goes there?" The sugar glider wove through the thin line of trees that framed the clearing, seeking out the strange voice.

"*Hola? Bonne nuit? Saluto?*" Bismark called out yet again. "Show yourself, shrieky stranger. Do not be scared. Come to your Papa Bismark!"

The others, too, were searching. Dawn circled the clearing's boundary and Tobin sniffed at dirt and roots, hoping to pick up a scent. When he failed to find anything, he lifted his head and called out into the dark.

"Hello?" The pangolin closed his eyes, listening closely for a reply. Normally, the valley was loud with the stirring of animals. But tonight, it was eerily quiet. Many creatures had left in search of food and water, and more were on their way out. Now, all Tobin could

17

hear were the sounds of the night—the low hum of the breeze, the crackling dry leaves, and the faint wisp of tumbleweeds sweeping over the grass.

"Any luck?" asked Dawn, joining Tobin near an old stump.

"Oh goodness," he sighed. "I'm afraid not."

"No luck here either," said Bismark, gliding next to the fox. "But nothing to worry about, I'm sure. You know..." he mused, turning to Tobin, "that sound probably was you after all. All that water sloshing around your guts." Bismark put his hands on his hips and shook his head from sid to side. "Tsk-tsk, *pangolino*. I told you to save some for *moi!*"

"Really, it wasn't me!" Tobin insisted. He blinked his eyes to clear his vision, which had suddenly grown blurry. "Maybe we're just imagining things," he said. "I do feel a bit faint from this heat." The pangolin pressed his eyes shut again and swallowed hard.

"Tobin, are you okay?" asked Dawn.

"Oh...oh goodness, yes," he replied. "I'm just a little...a little bit...*oof!*"

The woozy pangolin lost his balance, tipped backward and fell with a soft thud—onto a pile of dried grass and sticks.

Eeeeee!

Right as Tobin's rear hit the earth, a muffled shriek rang out again...and this time, it sounded like a cry of pain!

The pangolin quickly leaped to his feet and looked frantically every which way.

"Ah-ha! It *was* you!" Bismark shouted triumphantly, pointing at Tobin's rear. "I knew it! This better not be a sign that your stinker's about to blow!" The sugar glider plugged his tiny nose with one paw and fanned the air with the other.

"That wasn't me—I promise!" said Tobin. "I think the noise came from the forest."

Bismark scoffed, but the pangolin ignored his friend. He tilted his head toward the trees then gazed into their shadows. The forest was always dark, but tonight Tobin thought it felt even darker than usual. The pangolin gulped. Could some dangerous creature be lurking in the woods? Nervously, Tobin glanced back at his friends. "Something must be out there," he whispered.

"Come on, *muchacho*. We all heard it," said Bismark. "That noise came straight from your rear. It was as clear as the full moon! Dawn, *mon amour*, am I right?"

"It wasn't me," insisted the pangolin. "Really." But even the fox raised a questioning eyebrow. After all, she had heard the shriek come directly from Tobin's behind, too.

"Maybe our hearing isn't quite right. Maybe this dry weather is going to our heads," she said, trying to make Tobin feel better.

"Or our butts," Bismark muttered.

Tobin opened his mouth to protest. But before he could speak, a cry rang out.

"Help! Hellllpppp!"

Dawn's fur pricked on end. Bismark stood still as stone. And Tobin's scales began to tremble. This scream was different from the ones they'd just heard. The words were clear—someone was in trouble, and the voice sounded familiar.

Without a word, the animals drew out their glittering, blue snakeskin capes—the cloaks they wore when they took on a mission to save someone in danger. Within a moment, the capes were fastened securely around their necks. The Brigade was ready.

"This way," called Dawn. She was already on the

move, following the sound of the cry.

Tobin ran after her.

Bismark, however, scurried up the trunk of an elm tree then hopped out on a low-hanging branch. Proudly, he gazed down at his friends running into the forest. Then he puffed out his chest and called into the night, "We shall be bold in adventure! We shall be brave in challenge! The Nocturnal Brigade to the rescue!"

Chapter Three
TRAPPED

"Help! Help me!"

The voice cried out again—more urgent this time.

"It's coming from that den up ahead!" shouted Dawn, calling back to her friends. Despite her tired limbs and dry throat, the fox continued to race through the trees. But the night's heat was heavy, and her full speed was not nearly as fast as usual.

"Oh...goodness," huffed Tobin, trying to keep up.

"Come on Señor Slow-Scales!" Bismark yelled down from the treetops. "Pick up the pace like your buddy Bismark—macho marsupial, glider *extraordinaire*, flying wonder!"

Despite his thirst and fatigue, Tobin forced his legs to move faster. He raced through the dried brush and wove through the leafless trees. Finally, exhausted and breathless, the Brigade reached the den Dawn had seen.

Though its main chamber lay underground, the entrance was visible under a ledge of rock. It was framed with dried mud and sticks, but it had caved in. Now, it was just a heap of dry earth. What caused this den to collapse? they wondered.

"Help! Helllllp! Is somebody there?" the voice cried out again.

Tobin gasped. "Oh goodness! An animal is trapped inside!" He bent his snout toward the dirt. "We're coming!" he called. "Hold on!"

Dawn circled the den, searching for a different

way in. There was none. "We have no choice," she said. "We'll have to dig."

"Help!" the voice shrieked again. "Help me, please!"

Dawn and Tobin started to dig. Dawn loosened the dirt with her paws, and Tobin pierced and scooped it with his powerful claws.

Bismark, meanwhile, stood atop a small rock, a safe distance away from the dirty work. "Yes, *si*, good job, *amigos!*" he called, cupping his paws to his mouth. "Now just listen to me for some pointers. I will direct this rescue operation. My knowledge of engineering is unmatched, after all." Bismark cleared his throat. "First, we must support the wall to avoid cave-ins. Then we need to carry out the dirt. But most importantly—"

Dawn grunted and tried to ignore her friend.

When it came to messy or hard work, Bismark preferred the role of maestro—"overseeing" the work rather than doing it. But it really didn't matter. Since he was the size of a small chipmunk, he didn't have the strength to be of much help anyway.

"Dig! Dig! Dig!" Tobin urged himself on as he tunneled into the den at full speed.

"*Pangolino*! Dawn, *mon amour!* Do you hear me?" Bismark shouted. "You should really consider the brilliant strategies I am laying out for you. Under my leadership, we can accomplish this task so much more—*blegh!*" A clump of flying dirt smacked Bismark in the face, landing right in his wide-open yapper. "*Thwip-thwap-thwup,*" he sputtered, spitting it out.

"Good work, Tobin," said Dawn as the pangolin finished plowing through most of the soil. "We're almost there!" the fox called into the den.

"Okay!" A faint call rose from the chamber beneath the ground. Tobin's heart leaped in his chest. He knew that voice sounded familiar!

"It's Cora!" he gasped. Tobin looked at Dawn in alarm. It was the Brigade's beloved wombat friend. The pangolin's pulse quickened. Dawn's amber eyes widened. Then they started to dig again—harder and faster than ever.

"Don't worry, Cora!" called Tobin, clawing the earth. "We're coming!"

"*Oui*, we're coming!" echoed Bismark, still perched on his rock. But even the sugar glider could not just stand there and watch, knowing that it was Cora in need. And so, with a wave of his flaps, Bismark finally made his way forward and landed next to his fellow Brigade-mates. "Mademoiselle Cora!" he said, yelling over his digging friends. "Have no fear! I, Bismark, savior of the night, rescuer of wombats, am here! I shall save you!" And then he joined his friends…flicking a tiny bit of dirt with a single toe.

"I can see her!" Tobin cried as he and Dawn broke through the last of the dirt. They jumped through the opening and descended into the den.

"Cora!" Tobin clawed through a scratchy patch of tumbleweed and, at last, reached the wombat. Breathless, the pangolin bent down beside her. "Are you okay?" he asked.

The wombat could only sputter in reply. But it took just one look at her to know the answer. Her body was trembling, and her ribcage showed through her skin. Tobin wondered when she last had food or a drink.

Gently, the pangolin held Cora's face in his paws. Then he unfurled his long tongue and carefully licked the grime from her cheeks. Tobin smiled. Cora's fur was dull and her nose was chapped, but her eyes still glimmered like always. "Thank goodness we found you," he whispered.

Immediately, Cora brightened. Then, slowly, she inched her front paw forward until it was nestled in Tobin's claw.

The pangolin felt his scales tingle, and a warm, fuzzy feeling—the one he always seemed to get around Cora—spread from the top of his scaly head all the way down to his claws.

Dawn bent toward the wombat. "How did this happen?" she asked, eager to gather some information.

Cora swallowed hard. "I don't know," she said at last. She took a shallow breath. "It seemed to collapse out of nowhere!"

"It was probably from the drought," Dawn reasoned. "Mud can dry into brittle dirt and crumble." The fox circled the chamber, studying the walls that remained. "Your den's walls must have caked up, flaked off in pieces, then collapsed."

"That's probably what happened," Cora agreed. "It's just impossible to know for sure." The wombat picked up a clump of tumbleweed then tossed it aside. "This tumbleweed blew into my den by the bundle last night. I could barely even see through it!"

As Cora spoke, another piece of the odd tumbleweed rolled into the den.

"Goodness, it's everywhere," Tobin remarked.

Bismark scrunched his face in disgust. "I'll handle this one," he said. The sugar glider reeled back his puny leg. Then he kicked at the tuft of dried grass, plant stalks, and prickly fluff—but the ball clung to his foot. "*Blech!* Get it off me!" he shouted.

The sugar glider shook his foot in the air, flinging off most of the dry, grassy pieces. But one stick remained caught in his toes. "Oh no you don't!" he muttered. Bismark bent over and pawed at his foot. "Be gone!" he cried. "You nasty, icky, annoying, ugly…. Hmm." Suddenly, Bismark stopped his rant, tilted his head, and gazed down at the tumbleweed twig.

"This is actually a pretty fine stick," he said, plucking it from his toes. He swung the stick to and fro. "It's like a sword," he mused, "or a scepter!" Bismark thrust it into the air and proudly lifted his chin. "This stick really suits a royal creature like *moi*." Holding the stick high, the sugar glider marched a few paces, enjoying his regal act. Then, satisfied with his show, he tucked the stick in his flap for safekeeping. "Yes, a very fine stick indeed," he murmured.

Dawn hid a smile and turned her attention to Cora. "Is there anything else you can remember? Anything that might explain what happened to your den?"

Cora closed her eyes to concentrate. She sat silently for a few moments, thinking hard. "No," she finally said, opening her eyes. "I can't think of anything. Well...except for some strange noises."

Dawn's ears perked up. "What kind of strange noises?"

"I... I thought I heard cries," she whispered. "Strange, tiny cries. But..." Cora looked down, embarrassed. "But I didn't see anyone. No one was there."

Dawn, Tobin, and Bismark exchanged startled glances. *Were Cora's cries the same sounds they had heard earlier?*

"Were the cries high-pitched and squeaky?" Tobin asked.

"Um...I think so," she said. "Oh, but don't listen to me. I'm probably just hearing things. I've been so thirsty lately, I can't even tell what is what!" Cora let out a cracked, dry cough. Then she coughed again—louder, this time, and raspier. Unable to stop, she clutched her ribs and curled up on the den floor.

"Cora needs water badly," Tobin whispered. "We have to help her."

"I know where there's a watering hole," Dawn began, "but it's not nearby." The fox eyed Cora nervously. The wombat was very weak and the journey would be hot and long.

"Oh, Tobin," Cora whispered. "I…I don't know if I can make it."

"I do," said the pangolin. With a swivel of his scales and a quick swipe of his claw, Tobin cut off a small piece of his cape. Then he gently tied the blue snakeskin around Cora's thin wrist. "Now you can do anything!" he said, guiding the wombat out of the den.

"*Bueno.* Let's go," said the sugar glider. "Dawn said it's thataway." Bismark used his new stick to point east. "*Oui, mon amour?* Am I correct?"

"Yes." The fox looked at her friends and sighed. It was clear that the race to Cora's den, the hot, dry air, and the difficult digging had taken its toll. They all needed water badly. And Cora was so ill. Could they survive the journey?

Dawn straightened her spine, hiding her doubts from her friends. *We are the Nocturnal Brigade*, she told herself. *We've met tougher challenges.*

And so she set off with Bismark, Tobin and Cora behind her—unaware of just how tough their newest challenges would be.

Chapter Four
QUICKSAND

"Keep pumping those paws, *pangolino*!" yelled Bismark, waving his stick in the air. "The sooner we get to the watering hole, the sooner Mademoiselle Cora shall be restored to her once-lustrous self."

Tobin glanced at the wombat trudging slowly beside him. The group hadn't been walking for long, but she was already gasping and her legs were wobbly and weak.

"I'm...I'm going as fast as I can...." Tobin called, pretending to sound out of breath. He knew that he could move quicker, but he refused to leave Cora's side. "How much farther?" he asked. He paused so the wombat could rest.

Dawn raised her snout toward the night sky. The moon was hanging at its peak, high above the trees. That meant they had already been traveling for quite some time. But the watering hole was still a long way off.

"We'll get there by daybreak," said Dawn.

"*Mon dieu,* this journey is endless, I tell you! We might as well be traveling to the stars!" The sugar glider slouched, raised a flap to his forehead, and groaned. Then, noticing Dawn's raised brow, he quickly straightened. "Not that this is tough for *moi,* of course, *ma chérie.* And after all," he added, sidling up next to the fox, "I'd go to the ends of the earth for you, my lady."

"We'll be there soon enough," said Dawn.

"And there will be plenty to eat and drink once we get there!" added Tobin. He gave Cora an encouraging grin.

"That's right," said Dawn, nodding and smiling weakly. "Let's keep going."

"Indeed, *mi bella,*" agreed Bismark. "And I'll tell stories to pass the time!"

Ignoring his friends' rolling eyes, the sugar glider eagerly started to ramble.

"Shall I start with the time I defeated a snake with my own two paws?" he began. "It was no match for me, *amigos.* No match at all. Or how about that time I led us to victory against those crazy crocodiles? Or when I trapped a giant beast?" Bismark hopped and leaped through the dry grass and brown reeds, energized by his

34

own, mostly made-up feats. "Oh, so many glorious tales to tell." He sighed. "It's hard to choose where to start!"

For a while, Tobin, Cora, and Dawn endured the sugar glider's stories in silence. They were too hot and thirsty to chime in, ask him to stop, or challenge his exaggerated versions of his heroic deeds.

But soon enough, even Bismark's voice began to crack, fade, and finally cease. As they continued to walk, the air grew hotter, the land became drier and rougher, and more of the strange tumbleweeds came rolling in.

"*Oof!*" Tobin winced as a strand of it poked the skin between his claws. He stopped to pluck it free.

"Shouldn't we be close by now?" Cora asked, trying to catch her breath.

The pangolin gazed up. The sky was starting to brighten. Cora was right. The watering hole should have been in sight by now. But when Tobin looked across the land, all he saw were the dull browns and grays of dead shrubs. There was no sparkling water anywhere.

"Dawn?" Tobin called. "Are we…are we almost there?"

The fox paused. She had been wondering the same thing. "I thought it was closer than this," she said.

As she scanned the horizon looking for any familiar sight, she spotted something in the distance. It was a figure hanging from a tree.

Tobin narrowed his beady eyes and saw it, too. "Maybe that animal can tell us how much farther we need to go."

The group began to walk toward the stranger. As they drew closer, the creature lowered itself to the ground. It was a nine-banded armadillo—a fellow nocturnal with a long snout and rabbit-like ears.

"Oh goodness." Tobin gasped when he could see the armadillo clearly. Its eyes were wide and filled with fear. And its round, scaly body was pressed as tightly as possible against the trunk of the tree.

Dawn, too, saw the animal's strange behavior. Was it sick? Was there a predator nearby? "Everyone, stay back," she warned.

But Bismark, unaware of the armadillo's distress, jovially leaped toward it, determined to make a big entrance.

"Ahoy there, Señor Scale-Tail!" he shouted. "Come meet *our* scaly *compañero.*" He nodded over his shoulder to Tobin then looked back and forth between the pangolin and the armadillo, noting their similar, oblong shapes, short limbs, and taloned paws. "Hey, you two have a lot in common! Can you release a terrible stink from your rear end, too?" Warily, Bismark eyed the armadillo's backside. He plugged his nose before continuing to move closer.

"Oy!" The armadillo suddenly let out a shout. "Hold it right there, little feller—don't take another step! That there ground is a quagmire!" He pointed urgently toward a patch of sand just beyond Bismark's feet.

Bismark didn't know what a quagmire was, but he wasn't about to admit it... or seem afraid of it. So, with a confident grin, the sugar glider took a giant step forward.

The armadillo yelped and frantically waved his arms.

But Bismark dismissed him with a wave of his flap. "Don't be such a worrywart!" he cried. "This quigglemoo is no match for—" Suddenly, Bismark felt something under his paws. He looked down.

"AHHH!" The glider's already-bulbous eyes bulged even more. The earth was moving! The sand that was flat and still just moments ago was now churning around Bismark's feet...and sucking him under!

As the ground spiraled and swirled, the armadillo clutched his tree even tighter. "Get outer there!" he yelled. "Before yer a goner!"

Bismark urgently pumped his flaps, trying to lift himself out of the strange substance. But the more he moved, the more it pulled him in. "*Sacre bleu!*" he cried. "I can't move!"

Dawn's eyes widened. "It's quicksand!" she cried. "Bismark—stay still! It will get worse if you try to fight it!"

But the panicked sugar glider kept flapping and flailing. And sure enough, the more he did, the more the strange sand spun and sucked at his feet.

"Oh no!" Cora gulped. "He's sinking!"

"Hurry!" said Dawn, beckoning Tobin. "We

have to help him!" They bolted to the edge of the quicksand pit where Bismark continued to wriggle and writhe.

Dawn leaned over the swirling earth and stretched out a paw. "Grab on, Bismark!" she yelled. "Tobin, hold me tight."

Tobin quickly dug his back claws into the dirt, pressing them into the earth to make sure they wouldn't move. Then he grabbed onto Dawn's tail. "I've got you," he told her.

With Tobin's grip keeping her safe, Dawn reached farther out over the dangerous quicksand. But Bismark still couldn't grasp her paw.

"I'm a...*glug*...goner!" he shouted. The sand whirled around him like a tornado, drowning his voice and pulling him lower and lower. Bismark was now covered up to his chest.

"Tobin, we need to get closer!" yelled Dawn.

The pangolin looked down at his claws buried deep in the ground. He needed to yank them forward to get them out and move toward Bismark. But he needed to keep leaning backward if he was going to keep Dawn from falling into the quicksand. The pangolin took a deep breath. Then, very carefully, he wriggled his hind legs until they were free from the earth. "*Oof!*" Tobin allowed himself to fall on his rear so he could keep a firm hold on Dawn. Then, scooting on his scaled backside, Tobin inched his way closer to the strange, swirling sand.

"Hurry!" yelled Dawn.

Bismark kept sinking down into the goop. Now, only his eyes peeked over it as it twisted and twirled in thousands of flecks all around him.

"Almost ready!" huffed Tobin. "Just let me dig my claws back in...."

"I'm choking!" Bismark used all his strength to reach out to Dawn. With a mighty jerk, he grabbed onto her. But Tobin had not yet dug his feet into their new position—and the pangolin and the fox went tumbling forward into the quicksand with Bismark!

"Tobin!" cried Cora.

"Oy!" The armadillo buried his face in the tree bark—he could not bear to watch.

"Helllllp!" Bismark sputtered, managing to lift his head for a moment. But as quickly as it had surfaced over the sand, it sunk back beneath it.

"What do we do?" yelped Tobin. He struggled to rise above the swirling earth, but he couldn't move. He tried to curl his body into a ball—the position he took whenever he was frightened—but even that was impossible. He was totally stuck.

40

"Try to...try to...." Dawn's mind raced, but nothing she thought of—floating, swimming, steering, jumping—seemed possible. All around her, the earth churned and roiled in a violent sea of sand. It was as though millions of tiny fingers were grabbing hold of her fur and pulling her lower and lower.

The fox looked around frantically, struggling to peer through the spinning sand. She could no longer see Bismark. And all she could see of Tobin was the tip of his long, narrow snout. Helpless, she closed her eyes, shielding them from the sand whipping against her face. In moments, she would be fully buried beneath it.

But, all of a sudden, the sand stopped stinging her cheeks. The fox slowly opened her eyes. The quicksand's thrashing tornado had slowed into gentle waves. It was no longer trapping her. Dawn wriggled her paws—she could move! For a moment, she seemed to float, suspended in the strange sand. And then—

Thud.

Her body hit something hard. She was on the ground...and Bismark and Tobin were sprawled out beside her.

Tobin rubbed his sore scales. Then, slowly, he rose to his feet. "I can stand!" he exclaimed.

Bismark, too, managed to stand. "*Mon dieu!* I...I

41

did it!" he gasped. The sugar glider spat out a mouthful of sand. "I won! I defeated the dirt! I out-quicked the quicksand!"

"But...where did it go?" Tobin asked. He spun in a circle, searching for the swirling sand.

"It dissolved! Disappeared! Vanished!" Bismark exclaimed, poking the earth with his stick.

"No, it didn't," said Dawn. She pointed a paw overhead. "Look!"

The quicksand had lifted...and now drifted in the air. For a few moments, the flecks flurried in circles. Then they fluttered away with the breeze.

The trio stared at the flying quicksand in silence.

"Oy!" The armadillo finally opened his eyes and let go of his tree. "Are you three erright?" he asked. He trundled toward the Brigade. "I tried to warn yer—that there's a quagmire!"

The animal lowered his snout toward the ground to inspect it. "Or at least it was. I tell yer— that there slip-sand stuff keeps hap-nin' everywhere an armadillo turns... movin' this way and that. Comin' and goin'." He shuddered then pivoted back toward his tree. "The earth—she's comin' alive, I tell yer!" he shouted, scurrying away at full-speed. "She's tryin' to eat us dead!" Then, before the Brigade could ask any questions, he ran off into the woods.

"Did...did you hear that?" Cora reached for Tobin's paw. "Is he right? Is...is the earth really coming alive?"

Chapter Five
WHERES' THE WATER?

"The earth can't come alive. It's not possible…
right?" Tobin asked his friends.

"Of course it's possible!" Bismark declared,
waving his stick in the air. "It's the only explanation for
this madness. The earth is trying to swallow us!"

Tobin gulped. "But—"

"But yes, good point, *muchacho*. Perhaps it's
only trying to swallow *moi*. I *am* the biggest threat after
all—the most powerful, the most terrifying, the most
intelligent…and the most devastatingly handsome. It
makes perfect sense that the earth went after me first."
Bismark let out a sigh. "My greatness has put me in
danger. That's all there is to it."

Dawn's stern expression silenced Bismark,
but she had barely heard him to begin with. She was
absorbed in her own thoughts. The strange, sandy

earth they'd been trapped in had to be quicksand, she reasoned. But quicksand is wet, and they were in the middle of a drought. And quicksand wouldn't whip and thrash and rise up in the air. "None of this makes sense," Dawn said, her tawny brow furrowed.

"The land is going loco, *mes amis!*" said the sugar glider. "Totally loony, I tell you!"

The fox gazed at the horizon. It was nearly daybreak. They needed to continue on before the sun rose and the heat became too much to bear. "Let's go," she said.

As Dawn led the group through the plains, she replayed the quicksand incident over and over again, hoping to solve the puzzle. But no matter how hard she tried, she could not figure it out.

She looked back at her friends and let out a discouraged sigh. Tobin was now carrying Cora—she had gotten so weak that she could no longer walk. And with the wombat's weight on his back, the pangolin struggled, as well. Even Bismark had slowed, dragging his feet with each step. They needed something to keep them going—some sign, at least, that they were heading in the right direction.

The fox gazed at the surrounding dry fields and plants. A hill rose here and there along with some bare trees, but she did not recognize anything—until a tree up ahead came into view. Suddenly, she brightened.

"I recognize that tree," she said with confidence. The fox pointed to a large maple sitting on top of a hill. "The watering hole is just on the other side of that slope." She picked up speed and headed toward it.

With a determined flap, Bismark glided after the fox. Tobin trundled as fast as he could with the wombat on his back. Finally, breathless, the trio reached the hill's peak—and their hearts leaped with joy at what they saw. They had reached the watering hole.

Animals of all kinds were gathered around it. There were wallabies, rabbits, and mice. Possums, bilbies, and bandicoots. And there were flocks of different birds—hawks, falcons, and at least three species of owls. There were so many creatures there that they blocked the water from sight.

"*Mon dieu*, we're saved!" Bismark said gleefully. "Mother Nature has not abandoned her sweet children, after all. We'll be lapping up lovely liquid in no time!"

Tobin sighed with relief. It was so long since he'd had a real, full drink of water, he'd almost forgotten what it tasted like—but he was certain it would be wonderful. "We're here!" he whispered to Cora. "Everything's going to be fine."

But as the animals made their way down the hill and drew closer to the watering hole, things did not seem fine at all. Yes, there were plenty of animals gathered there, but the Brigade could now see that they were in terrible shape. The wallabies and possums were sprawled and moaning on the hot earth. The parched birds heaved with pained gasps and squawks. Some other animals lay still, making no noise at all.

"Oh goodness!" gasped Tobin.

For a moment, the Brigade stood in silence, shocked at the terrible sight before them. Then, slowly, they began to weave through the ill animals until they reached the line of dried reeds that circled the watering hole. Using her snout, the fox pushed the brittle plants aside, allowing the Brigade to reach the banks at last.

Dawn's jaw tightened as she gazed ahead of her. What she saw was not a watering hole at all. It was a dry pit, brown and empty, with a faint, chalky line where water had once met the banks. The only evidence of any water was a couple of small, muddy pools, and a few small fish—pale, gray, and still.

"Those poor animals," Tobin whispered.

Cora gave a weak nod, echoing the pangolin's thought.

"And poor us!" added the sugar glider, throwing

his flaps in the air in distress. "What are we supposed to do now?"

Dawn took a deep breath, hoping to loosen the tightness in her chest. "Before we do anything, Cora must take a sip of whatever water there is," she commanded.

Tobin carefully tilted his body so Cora could slide to the ground. Then he guided her to a small, murky puddle nearby. The weak wombat slowly lowered her mouth and lapped at the puddle. The few sips she managed to drink were dirty, hot, and not enough to help.

"Just stay here and rest," whispered Tobin.

The pangolin forced a warm smile before rejoining his Brigade-mates at the rim of the hole.

"I don't understand," murmured Dawn. She gazed down into the pit. "This watering hole was large—the size of a lake. Even with all these animals, there should still be plenty to drink."

"What are we going to do?" cried the sugar glider, grabbing hold of Dawn's leg. "What will become of us? What is our fate?" Bismark sighed. "I know! We're going to die, I tell you! Die! And what's worse…we'll die withered and wretched." He raised a flap to his forehead then gazed pleadingly up at Dawn. "Please, *mon amour,* just make me this tiny promise. When the crowds come to mourn me, don't let them see my dull eyes, dry fur, and chapped flaps! No—they must remember me at my finest!"

"Bismark," said the fox sharply. "There's no time for this. We need to find out where all the water has gone. And why."

"Well that's precisely—*ahem*—what I want to know," a gruff voice said

The Brigade-mates spun around at the unfamiliar voice somewhere within the reeds. Then, parting the plants with his webbed feet, a platypus emerged.

"Oh *mon dieu,*" Bismark gasped. "I know not

everyone can be as handsome as the sugar glider, but this is horrible, misshapen, hideous!"

Dawn glared at Bismark. But she had to admit, the platypus was a strange-looking creature. In fact, it looked like many creatures in one. His feet were webbed like a frog's, but they also had claws, like a lion's. And though he had fur and a tail like a beaver, his snout resembled a duck's bill.

"Look all you want—*ahem,*" the platypus coughed. "But there's no water here. It disappeared after I came."

"What do you mean 'disappeared'?" asked Dawn.

The platypus let out something between a sneeze and a cough then shook his bill from side to side. "Well—ahem—the watering hole was fine when I got here. Low, but still fine." He snorted. "But a few nights ago," he continued, "it started to disappear—and fast. Before we knew it, it was all gone!"

Dawn narrowed her eyes. "I don't understand," she said. "An entire watering hole can't just vanish in a few nights. There must be a logical explanation for this."

"Indeed, there must," agreed Bismark. "So fear not, everyone. With my brilliant powers of detection, I will solve this mystery before you can say 'magnificent marsupial!'"

With a whoosh of his cape, Bismark set off, flapping his way through the reeds. "*Pangolino*, come help me!" he called. "Sniff around with that schnoz of yours. We must search for clues."

While Tobin and Bismark explored, Dawn stood on the edge of the bank. Her mind raced as she thought about the unusual events of the night: first, noises, unfamiliar and out of nowhere. Then, quicksand, sucking them down then suddenly drifting away. And now, water that had simply vanished.

She narrowed her eyes. *What could possibly account for these bizarre occurrences?* she asked herself. *What is going on?* With her thoughts still spinning, the fox paced around the water's edge, joining her friends in their search. But she could not help but wonder: What would they find next?

Chapter Six
THE VANISHING CHUTE

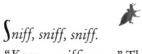*niff, sniff, sniff.*

"Keep...sniffing...." The pangolin panted. After searching all the weeds around the watering hole, Tobin paused on the bank and rubbed his exhausted snout. Then he trudged toward the sugar glider who had also stopped. "Oh goodness, Bismark," he sighed. "I've sniffed everywhere and I haven't found a single clue."

But Bismark did not reply. His bulbous eyes were fixed on the far side of the watering hole where Dawn was still searching the ground.

Tobin cocked his head. "Do you see something?" he asked.

"Just my one true love," Bismark swooned, keeping his gaze on the fox. "Even in dark times, my *bella* Dawn remains a source of bright light."

Tobin sighed. The sky was growing pale. Soon,

the night would be over. And still, they had no water and no idea where to find some. Discouraged, the pangolin glanced back at Cora, resting in the dry crater. *How can I return to her with nothing good to report?* he wondered. Then Dawn's voice rang out. "I found something!" she shouted, and Tobin's heart leaped with hope.

"What is it, milady?" shouted Bismark as he and Tobin ran to her.

"Look," whispered the fox.

Past her paws lay a curved chute. It reminded Tobin of a watermelon, cut in half and hollowed out. Except it was made of vines, sticks, and leaves. And a small trickle of water ran through it.

"In the name of sweet fruit—we are saved!" Bismark threw his flaps open with joy and wrapped them around Dawn's leg. "Fear not, *mi bella*—we shall live on and enjoy a long future together as planned!"

But Dawn did not seem to share Bismark's enthusiasm about their "future" or the chute with the trickle of water. Freeing herself of the glider, the fox moved forward to inspect it more closely. "I almost didn't see it because it blends right into the forest floor," she said. "Someone made it."

Tobin tilted his head in confusion. "Made it for what?" he asked.

"I'm not sure," she said. Slowly, Dawn paced alongside the chute. She could see now that it was quite long and led into the forest...but where did it begin?

Suddenly, the fur on Dawn's spine stood on end. *Could it be?* she wondered.

Without saying a word, the fox dashed back to the rim of the watering hole, with Tobin and Bismark close behind.

"What is it, *mon amour?*" Bismark asked. "What is so alarming?"

Dawn pointed to the bottom of the bank. "The chute begins here—right at the edge of the watering hole," she said. "Someone used it to drain out the water!"

"*Sacre bleu!*" Bismark exclaimed.

Tobin shook his head, bewildered. "Who would do this?" he cried. "Who would steal all the water?"

"I'll tell you who," Bismark said, his voice growing loud and high-pitched. "It was a monster! A devil! A burrowing barbarian!" he yelled, flailing his flaps in the air. Then, overcome with frustration, he angrily pulled out his walking stick and whipped it against a stone.

Eeeeee!

"Oh goodness!" Tobin exclaimed. "I just heard it again—the high-pitched shriek!"

"*Mon dieu*—another poof, *pangolino*?" Bismark scrunched his nose in disgust.

"It wasn't me!" Tobin insisted.

"Oh please, *por favor,* stop denying it. There's nothing else it could be—besides, perhaps, the whistle of my wondrous flaps as I whacked my stick."

Bismark looked down at his stick and gasped. "No!!!" A small piece of it had broken off when he'd hit it against the rock. "*Mon dieu!* Just when you think things can't get worse," he wailed, cradling his now-shortened stick. With a sigh, Bismark tucked it back in his flap. Then he admired his feeble arm muscles. "I must not know my own strength," he remarked. "And I'll only grow stronger once I get my paws on the water that has been stolen!"

Bismark spread his flaps, preparing to follow the length of the chute to see where it went. But Dawn held up a paw. "Not yet," she said. "There isn't much water here. Only a small stream is left. We need to let Cora drink before we keep going."

Tobin raced to the wombat and carried her to the chute. Then, he gently lowered her to the ground. As she slid down his side, his stomach twisted in knots. Cora was so thin now, he could feel her bones on his scales. But when she peered over the edge of the chute at the trickle of water, Tobin felt a rush of joy.

Slowly, with her eyes closed, Cora lowered her face and opened her mouth to drink.

Whoosh!

The moment her tongue touched the chute, it broke into pieces—then the pieces flew into the air!

The Brigade jumped back in shock as bark and dry leaves fluttered and swirled around their heads. Vines and sticks twisted and thrashed mid-air, then lifted higher and higher until they flew away. What had looked like a solid chute on the ground an instant ago was now a forest frenzy in flight!

"Great Scott!" Bismark shouted, swatting the leaves and sticks hitting his face. "It's alive! It's another conundrum, a mystery, a flapdoodle!"

"Oh goodness!" cried Tobin. "We have to

catch it. We have to get it back!" Desperately, Tobin began to claw at the fragments swirling over his head, hoping to knock some down to catch some drops of water.

Dawn and Bismark joined in, the fox batting at the air with her paws, and the sugar glider leaping up with flaps opened wide, attempting to use their folds as a trap.

But their efforts failed. In a matter of moments, all the pieces had flittered away, and the water had disappeared—rising and evaporating in a fine mist, or seeping into the hot, parched ground with a sizzle.

The animals stood there, panting and perplexed. Just like that, the chute was gone—vanishing as if it had never been there at all.

Chapter Seven
THE MIRAGE

"Did you see that, *amigos?*" yelped Bismark. "Someone booby-trapped that water to flap me silly!"

"Oh goodness!" cried Tobin. "What…what just happened?"

Completely baffled, Tobin, Bismark, and Cora looked to Dawn for an explanation, but she could only shake her head in bewilderment.

How could this be possible? She desperately wanted to comfort her friends with a logical explanation, but she couldn't think clearly. The fox blinked her amber eyes hard. Her head was throbbing from confusion. Did she really see what she thought she saw?

The fox began to pace as she thought about it some more. She paused and looked at her friends. "Yes," she muttered. "It's the only thing that makes sense. What we just saw must have been a mirage—a hallucination," she declared, her voice gaining certainty. "Extreme thirst can make you see all kinds of things that aren't really there. I thought only desert animals saw mirages, but we've never had a drought this bad before."

"Seeing things that aren't there? Oh goodness!" gasped Tobin. "Could we really be going crazy from dehydration?"

"*Dios mio!*" cried Bismark. "This drought is making us loco! Loony! Lopsided!" He tugged at his fur in distress. "Before long, our brains will turn into bat poo. Bat poo, I tell you!"

Tobin let out a yelp.

"It's horrifying, *amigo,* I know," said Bismark. "What would the world do without my superior brainpower? My incredible intellect? My glorious noggin? Animals everywhere would be lost, I tell you! Helpless! Deprived!"

But Tobin was focused on the wombat, not the sugar glider. With no warning at all, Cora had collapsed!

Tobin rushed to her side. "Cora!" he cried. "Cora…can you hear me?" Carefully, the pangolin lifted the wombat's head and cradled it in his lap. After a few moments, Cora's eyes fluttered open.

"Oh…oh no…what happened?" she whispered.

"You fainted, *amiga!*" cried Bismark, gliding

60

next to the wombat. "You're even weaker and woozier than I thought!"

Dawn met Tobin's worried gaze. "We'll have to let Cora rest here while we search for water," she said softly. "She's too weak to travel."

The fox looked up at the night sky. The cool blues were shifting to the warmer, rosy colors of morning. The sun would be rising shortly. "Cover Cora with leaves," she told the pangolin. "We need to keep her out of the sun until we return."

Tobin felt a pang in his stomach. He hated the idea of leaving Cora, especially now. But the wombat had grown much worse. Her legs could no longer hold her weight, her breathing had gotten shallower, and her eyes no longer shone with their usual cheerful glimmer. Tobin sighed—he knew his leader was right. They had to keep searching for water, and the wombat was too frail to join them.

Sadly, Tobin trudged toward the brush and began to gather dried leaves...but he could not hold onto what he picked up. "Oh goodness," he sighed. Each time he collected a bundle of leaves, they seemed to fly right out of his claws!

"Hurry up, *mon ami!*" shouted Bismark, impatiently tapping his stick. "Cover Cora, and let's get going!"

"I'm trying!" called Tobin.

The pangolin grabbed some more leaves, this time holding them with an extra-firm grasp until he set them on top of the wombat. But by the time he came back with more, the first batch had flitted away.

This doesn't make sense, Tobin thought. *Cora's not moving and there's no breeze. There's nothing to blow these leaves out of place.*

Tobin gathered another pile of leaves and blanketed Cora with them. Again, they scattered. "Oh goodness," he said with a frustrated sigh. "I've never seen leaves like this. Nothing is right. Nothing is happening the way it should." He took a deep breath and tried again, scooping up more leaves and placing them on Cora. But once more, they quickly fluttered away.

What was going on? Tobin wondered. Was this another mirage? Was he so hot, hungry, and tired that he was imagining this? Or was the platypus right—was the earth really coming alive? His heart started to pound at the thought.

"*Mon dieu, muchacho!* Pick up the pace!" called Bismark. "I could harvest pomelos faster than this!"

Tobin drew in a breath and kept working. Finally, he had accumulated a pile of dry leaves so large, that even if half disappeared, the wombat would still remain covered.

The pangolin crouched next to Cora. "We'll be back soon," he whispered, brushing her cheek with his paw.

Cora looked up at Tobin with dry, bloodshot eyes. She was too weak to reply. But with her last bit of strength, she moved just enough to give him an affectionate nudge with her nose. Then, almost immediately, her lids closed and she dozed off with a light snore.

With one final glance at the wombat, Tobin left to join his Brigade-mates. "She'll be safe now," he said, but his heart continued to race with fear.

"Oh, don't worry, *compadre*," said Bismark, throwing a flap around Tobin. "Your little *señorita* will be just fine." But when he looked at the pangolin, his jaw dropped. "Holy glider!" he cried. "What was that?"

With his bulbous eyes bulging in horror, the sugar glider stepped up to the pangolin, examining the scales on his back. He could have sworn he'd seen a couple of them detach from his friend and fly off! But no, he thought. *That's just crazy!* Bismark sighed and massaged his tiny temples in distress. *My sweet fox is right—we're seeing things that aren't there. I need water more than I thought!*

"What's wrong, Bismark?" asked Tobin.

But before the sugar glider could answer, Dawn held up a paw.

"Everyone, shh!" she whispered. "I think I hear something." The fox's ears pricked on end as she listened again. *Could it really be?* she wondered.

She closed her eyes, craned her neck, and listened one more time. Yes. It was unmistakable. "Water—I hear rushing water!" she said, her eyes flickering. "This way!"

And then, with a leap and a whoosh of her tail, she was off, leading the Brigade toward the sound.

Chapter Eight
LYRE! LYRE!

"Pardon me, *ma chérie*, but I think your thirst is playing tricks on you," called Bismark, gliding after the fox. "I hear nothing—*nada!*"

Tobin didn't hear anything either but, like Bismark, he was loyal to Dawn, so he followed her without question. He felt lighter now, without Cora's weight on his back. His progress was hampered, however, by the thick balls of tumbleweeds that started rolling his way.

"Oh goodness, how can you two get anywhere with all this mess?" Tobin asked. No matter where he went, the tumbleweeds seemed to follow, blocking his path.

"*Oof!*" The pangolin batted a clump twice his size with his claw. But as soon as it rolled away from him, another tumbleweed came bounding toward him, almost knocking him down!

Tobin leaped to the right, trying to dodge the hay-like ball. But when he veered to the side, so did the tumbleweed. Quickly, Tobin changed direction, leaping left to avoid it. But then the tumbleweed leaped left as well!

"Oh goodness!" cried Tobin. "This tumbleweed has a mind of its own! I know it's not possible—but I think it's following me!"

"That's doubtful, *muchacho*," said Bismark, glancing back at his friend. "Nothing—not even that nasty weed ball—would risk following you!" He eyed Tobin's rear end and laughed.

"*Mon amour!*" he shouted to Dawn. "Are you sure you heard rushing water? We could be running full speed after some imaginary sound!" He sighed. "Do you hear it, *pangolino*?"

Tobin shook his head no.

"I heard it," Dawn said, still racing through the forest. "There must be water nearby."

Bismark and Tobin shared a fretful look. They rarely doubted their leader. She was always so wise and reliable, but they were losing their confidence with this senseless chase.

"Oh goodness!" Suddenly, Tobin stopped and cocked his head. "Listen, Bismark! I think I do hear something!" He listened again. "Yes! Yes! I hear rushing water!"

Bismark cupped a paw to his ear. After a few moments, his eyes lit up. "I hear it, too!" he agreed. "Oh, my sweet fox," he sang, gliding along Dawn's side, "I'm sorry I ever doubted you. You're not crazy, after all! Crazy for my love, maybe, but not crazy in the head."

Dawn's lips curled in a small grin. "Let's just keep going," she said.

The Brigade moved faster now, the sound of the water renewing their strength. As they approached a clearing, the splashing grew louder and louder.

"The water must be just through these trees!" said Tobin eagerly.

The animals raced toward the noise, but when they arrived at the clearing's edge, Dawn skidded to a halt.

Whoosh, splish, splash, gurgle.

The clearing was filled with the sounds of a babbling brook. But there was no water in sight.

"Where...where is it?" asked Tobin. The pangolin squinted, studying his surroundings, but he saw only dry grass.

69

Tobin moved into the clearing. He knew his eyesight was poor; perhaps his strong sense of smell would be more helpful. Closing his eyes, the pangolin pointed his snout left and right, up and down, sniffing the hot air. But he could not detect any mossy, muddy, or watery smells at all.

While Tobin sniffed through the grass, Bismark glided from branch to branch, hoping to spot water from above. Dawn, meanwhile, searched the clearing's borders.

"Do you see anything?" asked the pangolin, calling out to his friends. He hoped that they were having better luck than he was.

But both the sugar glider and the fox had found nothing.

"*No comprendo!*" wailed Bismark. "It doesn't make any sense! The sound of water is everywhere, but the *sight* of water is nowhere. Nowhere, I say!"

Indeed, the splish-splashing sounds of water continued to fill the air.

"Oh goodness, I don't understand!" said Tobin.

"I can't stand this forest trickery any longer!" Bismark shouted. He covered his ears with his flaps to block out the watery noise. "*Mon dieu!* Be gone, sounds of insanity! For the love of all gliders, be gone!"

Then, all at once, the whooshing, gurgling sounds ceased.

Slowly, Bismark removed his flaps from his ears, and for a moment, the Brigade stood in dumbfounded silence. Then, sounds rang through the clearing again. But this time, it wasn't water the animals heard—it was a voice:

"Oh goodness!"

"*Mon dieu!*"

"Be gone!"

The Brigade exchanged looks of alarm. Their own words were ringing through the clearing...but neither Dawn, nor Tobin, nor Bismark was speaking!

"*Quoi?* Who said that?" Bismark shouted into the darkness.

"*Quoi?* Who said that?" echoed the voice.

Tobin felt his belly tighten with fear. Now what was happening? "Who...who's there?" he asked.

"Who's there?" said the voice.

"How dare you mock us?" cried Bismark. The sugar glider stepped forward boldly, wielding his stick in his paw. "Come forward at once!" he demanded. "Show yourselves, you crowing cowards, you repeating pests!"

"Crowing cowards!"

"Repeating pests!"

"I don't even sound like that!" Bismark protested, placing his paws on his hips. "That voice is far too obnoxious!"

"Too obnoxious! Too obnoxious!"

Dawn circled the area, sniffing and listening as the voices continued to call out. "They're coming from over there," she said, pointing at a cluster of oak trees framing the clearing's far side. "This way!"

With Dawn in the lead, the Nocturnal Brigade crossed the clearing. But when they reached the oaks, they found no one.

"Show yourself, you mimicking fool!" Bismark shouted, stomping his feet in frustration.

"Mimicking fool! Mimicking fool!"

The fox padded into the cluster of trees and searched their branches.

On a low-hanging limb, three birds were perched over their heads. Each of them had a long, graceful neck and a strong, powerful beak. But the birds' outstanding feature was their feathers. Their bodies were solid black, but their long feathered tails stretched far behind them in striking patterns of orange and blue.

"Lyrebirds," said Dawn. "Of course! They mimic whatever sound they've most recently heard."

"So these are the culprits?" asked Bismark. "These birds are the ones who are mocking us?"

"Yes." Dawn kept her eyes on the birds. "They mimicked our words because they heard our voices. And before that, they were mimicking the sound of rushing water…"

"… because they must have heard water nearby!" finished Tobin.

"Nearby!" The lyrebirds echoed back. "Nearby!"

"Exactly," confirmed the fox.

"*Mon dieu!* At long last—with these birdies' help, we shall drink!" exclaimed Bismark.

The fox treaded closer to the birds until she stood directly below them. "Where is the water?" she asked, looking up.

Anxiously, the Brigade-mates awaited the birds' reply…but all that came back was more mimicry.

"Oh goodness!"

"*Mon dieu!*"

"Where is the water?"

Dawn growled in frustration, shaking her head. "These birds can't hold a real conversation. They can only repeat."

"But I'm so thirsty...." Tobin's voice cracked. He swallowed hard. Then, disappointed and fatigued, the pangolin slumped to the ground. "I thought we'd found water."

"We'll never find water," Bismark grumbled bitterly. "These birdbrains are a dead end!"

"Never find water."

"Never find water."

The lyrebirds continued to mimic the Brigade. Then they spread their short wings and lifted off their branches. As they jumped their way from branch to branch, the Brigade could hear their voices echoing through the woods.

'Dead end...."

'Dead end...."

'Dead end...."

74

Chapter Nine
BARK BITES

"There's no time to waste—we need to follow them!" Dawn ran after the lyrebirds. "They've been near water—and I bet they'll return to it."

"Oh goodness!" cried Tobin, setting off after the fox. "This is how we'll finally get water. We can't lose them!"

But before long, that's exactly what happened— the Brigade lost track of the birds.

"Have no fear, *amigos*," said Bismark, valiantly swirling his stick. "There's *nada* to be concerned about. This is a job for the only—and, might I add, magnificent—flyer in our little search party—*moi!* I will scout from above and find those birdies before you can say 'lyre lyre.'"

Bismark waved his stick once more and set it at the base of a tree trunk, propping it against the bark.

Then he extended his flaps, caught the warm breeze, and glided up to the tree's first low limb.

Tobin gazed after his friend and squinted at the tree. Although his eyesight was lacking, he could tell that the tree did not look quite right. "Oh goodness, Bismark. I think you should come down."

Bismark climbed higher then peered down at Tobin, who was cradling his stomach with worry. "Oh *amigo,* are you gonna blow?" The sugar glider plugged his nose. *"Por favor,* don't be afraid. I've climbed trees millions of times! There's nothing to be scared of here... except for your pungent poof."

Tobin sighed. "I'm not going to—" But the pangolin's voice dropped off at the sight of something just above his friend. There was something wrong with the tree. It was moving! The top of the trunk had begun to ripple in waves.

"Bismark, look out!" he screamed. Frantically, he waved his claw at the tree. "The bark! It's... it's alive! You have to get out of there!"

But the sugar glider just rolled his eyes. "Can't you see, *muchacho?* You're falling for another mirage! Now, just sit and calm down," he advised. "You just need to—*mon dieu!"* Bismark caught sight of the tree bark over his head shifting, jiggling, and pulsing on the

trunk. Then, suddenly, the bark beneath Bismark's paws began to fly off. And as it fell away from the tree, so did the sugar glider.

"*Ahhhhhh!*" Bismark cried as he started to tumble to the ground.

Desperately, he reached out toward the tree, hoping to grab it and stop his fall. At last, he managed to dig his small claws into its trunk. But just as he gained a good hold of it and caught his breath, the bark there flew off, too! Then, like a swarm of bees, it circled him—and attacked.

"Help me! It's stinging me!"

"Bismark!" Dawn yelled. "Get away from that tree! NOW!"

Bismark leaped from the trunk and glided to the tree next to it. "Phew!" He sighed. "That was a close one! I almost—*ahhhh!*" Bismark felt a sharp pinch, then a sharper one. He let out a panicked yelp. This tree's bark had come alive, too—and it was trying to bite him!

"The wilds have gone wild!" shrieked Bismark. "This tree is trying to kill me!"

Desperately, the sugar glider scrambled higher into the tree, trying to escape the vicious bark.

But at the top, the attack grew stronger. Now, sharp pieces of wood pierced Bismark's flaps, trying to nail him to the tree. "*Eeeeeek!*" he screeched.

"You have to find a way to get down!" shouted Dawn.

But flail and flop as he might, Bismark could barely move. "I'm trying, *mon amour,* but the tree won't let me!" The sugar glider gazed down at his Brigade-mates and waved good-bye with his paw. "Farewell, my friends, *adios, mes amis!*" he blubbered. "The earth has finally succeeded where so many have failed! I'm a goner. This is the end—OOF!"

Something was twisting around Bismark. What

was this new horror? He gasped as a
vine slowly crept around his body
It circled his legs then moved up to
his stomach. "What are you doing?"
he cried. "Release me at once!"

But the vine just grew
tighter and tighter as it wound its way
up Bismark's body. It was up to his
neck now, squeezing against his throat,
making it hard for him to breathe. The sugar glider
clutched at the vine, pulling on it frantically, desperate
to loosen its hold.

As the vine tightened around him, Bismark's
vision began to grow dark. "Help…" he wheezed. His
eyelids began to droop. Then, he heard a faint sound.

Heh, heh, heh.

The sound of someone snickering!

Is someone laughing at me? Bismark wondered.
*Mon dieu! Have I died and gone to some strange place
where I'm laughed at instead of admired?*

Bismark felt himself moving. The vine pulled
him back, then—*snap!* With a sharp jolt, it hurled the
sugar glider through the air like a stone from a slingshot.

On the forest floor below, the pangolin and the

fox watched in horror as their friend went sailing far into the distance…over the trees and out of sight.

For a moment, Tobin and Dawn stood silent, listening for their friend's voice to call out. But they didn't hear anything—no cries, no shouts, no screams.

The pangolin felt a horrible wave of nausea wash over him. Was Bismark…?

Splash!

Startled, Dawn and Tobin jumped. Could it be? Had Bismark landed in water?

The friends took off at once, racing through the woods to find out.

Chapter Ten
SPLASH!

"Bismark! Bismark! Where are you?" Tobin shouted.

The pangolin and fox raced through the forest as fast as they could, desperate to find their friend.

How far had those strange vines flung him? Was he hurt? Could he really have landed in water? Bismark couldn't swim, and Tobin's mind reeled with all the terrible possibilities. They had to reach him quickly — but that was proving quite difficult. The tumbleweeds had multiplied. They were everywhere now, rolling from all directions and blocking the animals' path. Dawn was agile and managed to leap over and around them. But Tobin was having more trouble.

"Oh…oh goodness," he panted. The pangolin's breath was short, his legs were tired, and his snout was itchy from the weeds. All he wanted to do was curl up and close his eyes, but he knew he had to keep going. So he forced himself onward, churning his powerful claws and swinging his scaly tail until the trees thinned, giving him more room to dodge the terrible tumbleweeds. At last, he caught up to Dawn. But still, there was no sign of Bismark.

Splash!

"We're coming, Bismark!" Tobin shouted, following the sound.

The pangolin and the fox arrived at the edge of a clearing, but aside from dried brush and weeds, there was nothing to see.

Confused, they moved forward past a cluster of dried brush—and then they laughed.

In front of them was a small pond. A very small pond—actually, more like a large puddle. But it was water, just the same. And right in the middle of it was Bismark, splashing and frolicking with glee.

"There you two are!" he shouted, spotting Tobin and Dawn. *"Mon dieu!* Did you see me defeat those treacherous trees? That bark tried to butcher me, but look!" The sugar glider stood in the pond, gathered water in his flaps, and tossed it high in the air. "I found the new watering hole!" he announced as the droplets showered down on him. "Case closed, *compadres!* Water discovered. I've saved the night!"

"Oh goodness, Bismark." Tobin sighed with relief and moved toward the pond's edge. "I'm glad you're all right."

"And you, my sweet? Are you happy to see me?" Bismark asked Dawn.

"Yes, I am," she said, her mouth curling into a small smile. "But I wouldn't call this a watering hole, Bismark. It looks more like a watering *puddle.*" Dawn reached into the water, testing its depth. It barely covered her paw. "That's hardly enough to satisfy one animal."

But Bismark wasn't listening. He was preoccupied by the sight of his reflection in the water's surface. "I haven't seen myself in so long," he said with a sigh. "Oh, how I've missed the sight of my fabulous face!" He scooped a handful of water onto his head, smoothing back his fur. "Good glider, I'm handsome." He swooned.

"I'm glad you're enjoying yourself," Dawn said, rolling her eyes.

"He certainly is happy," Tobin said.

Bismark grinned, blowing a kiss to Dawn. "I'm sure you must be happy, too, my beautiful, tawny true love—to see the object of your affection returned to his dashing self."

"I'm glad you're okay," said Dawn, "but there's still work to be done. There's barely enough water here to keep the three of us going, and there's definitely not enough to cure Cora and all those other sick animals."

At the mention of Cora's name, the pangolin's stomach tightened into knots. Tobin looked up at the sky, blue with the light of the morning. They had left her all alone. *How was she?* he wondered. *How much longer could she last?*

"What should we do?" he asked, cradling his belly.

"We need to continue to search for the water," said Dawn. "But in the meantime, we need to drink. If we don't, we won't be of use to anyone."

Tobin nodded. Together, he and Dawn lowered their heads toward the shimmering pool.

"*Dios mio!*" cried Bismark. At once, the sugar glider leaped out of the water, pushed past his friends, and ran toward a stick on the shore. "Look!" he exclaimed, clapping his paws with delight. "It's my stick! It's here!" Triumphantly, the sugar glider started a victory march back toward his friends, waving at them with his stick.

Tobin slowly waved back at Bismark, his brow furrowed in confusion. "If that's Bismark's stick, how did it get here?" he asked Dawn.

"It couldn't have," she answered, shaking her head.

"Oh, what friends you are!" Bismark cried, smiling at his Brigade-mates, then hugging one of Dawn's legs. "You remembered to bring my stick! It touches my heart. You know how much this stick means to me."

Tobin coughed uncomfortably.

"What's wrong, *mi amigo?* Is your throat dry?" Bismark asked. "Well, that's not a *problemo* anymore! Just have a drink at my private water source, Lake Bismark! It's the least I can do after you so thoughtfully brought me my stick. You, too, my darling Dawn. Imbibe the sparkling waters of my glorious namesake. Guzzle, drink, and be merry!"

Dawn shook her head. It was impossible for Bismark's stick to appear here. And yet, here it was.

The fox watched Tobin eagerly lap up water

with his long tongue. She smiled then lowered her snout to do the same. Perhaps the water would clear her mind in addition to quenching her thirst. As soon as her lips touched the pool's surface, the fox's tense muscles relaxed. And as she slowly drank, she could feel life coursing back through her veins. Dawn closed her eyes, enjoying the moment.

When she finished, her limbs still felt weak and her fur was still dry, but her body felt stronger and her mind felt sharper. "Bismark," she said. Her voice was clearer now. "We did not bring that stick along. I'm certain we left it behind."

"Yes," agreed Tobin, licking drops off his snout then coiling his tongue in his belly. "It's probably still at the tree where you left it."

But Bismark did not respond. He just stared at his stick with narrowed eyes.

"Bismark, are you okay?" Tobin asked.

"*C'est impossible,*" Bismark said, scratching his bald spot. "How can this be explained?" Bewildered, he looked up at his friends. "Do you remember when a piece of my stick came off due to my supreme strength?" he asked.

"Um...sure," stammered Tobin.

"Well, look! It's not gone anymore. The piece

86

that broke off has grown back!" Bismark stared at the stick in awe. "There is no end to the remarkable things this stick can do," he continued. "It found me here even though I left it behind, and now it has repaired itself. Oh, stick!" he cried, hugging it to his chest. "You are marvelous, miraculous, *magnifique!* We really are meant for each other."

"Oh goodness, Bismark…are you sure this is your stick?" Tobin asked carefully. "It just doesn't make sense for it to end up here…or to repair itself. It's probably a different stick," he offered, nervously eyeing his friend. "A new, really wonderful one!"

"How dare you? Of course I'm sure it's my stick!" The sugar glider shielded his prized possession with his flap, as though he were protecting it from Tobin's words. Then he gazed down at the stick and stroked its bark with his paw. "Look at all its unique traits," he said. "The knobby thing near the top…the darker part at the end…and see? These are the little prongy parts sticking out from the sides." Bismark lifted his chin proudly, as though he had proven his point without doubt. "I told you! There's no other stick like it. It's one of a kind, I tell you—like *moi!*"

"Okay," Dawn said, with more than a hint of uncertainty, "but no matter which stick this is, we cannot stay here admiring it. We have to find water for Cora before the sun fully rises and the heat of day sets in."

"Oh goodness. Poor Cora," Tobin fretted.

"Indeed," agreed Bismark. "Now let's go—there's no time to lose! The sooner I find this *agua*, the sooner I'll be adored for it." The sugar glider thoughtfully cradled his chin. "Hmm," he murmured. "How shall I be commemorated for yet another astounding accomplishment? With a party, perhaps? A feast?"

"Bismark," Dawn chided. "The water is what's important."

"But of course!" exclaimed Bismark. "That's it! A water fountain in my honor! You're a genius, milady." The sugar glider's eyes glistened as he pictured the sight. "It will be striking, towering, grand! Obviously, it will feature a statue of me, just slightly larger than life-size… about the height of a tree. And the water will spout from my—"

"Bismark!"

The sugar glider jumped at the fox's sharp tone. "Forgive me, my love. I got distracted by your magnificent idea." With a flourish, Bismark flung his wet cape over his shoulders, spraying Tobin and Dawn. Then he extended his stick out in front of him. "Lead us on, stick!" he cried, grasping it with both hands. "Take us to water! If any stick can do it, it's you."

Stumbling forward, acting as though the stick were pulling him, Bismark led the way. "Wheeee! The stick is on the trail!" he shouted excitedly.

"Do you think that stick can really find water?" Tobin asked Dawn.

The fox sighed. It was an absurd notion, but she resisted her urge to say so. The truth was, she couldn't say "no" with certainty. Stranger things had already happened.

Chapter Eleven
BLACK MAGIC

The morning sun had risen higher in the sky. Its strong rays beat down on the animals. "I don't know what to say, *amigos.*" Bismark sighed, wiping sweat off his bald spot. "Despite my stick's earlier feats, it has now fumbled, faltered, and failed us. It hasn't found a drip-drop of water. It's just led us to more of these— *oomph!*—stupid tumbleweeds!" Bismark let out a grunt as he booted the fuzzy ball to the side.

Tobin watched a few dry, withered leaves float down from the trees and swatted a tumbleweed out of his way, too. *What's happening to our forest?* he wondered, squinting in the bright light. He thought of all the baffling things the trio had come across—mysterious voices, the churning ground, the vanishing chute, swirling tree bark, disappearing water.... The pangolin gulped. "Everything that has happened is so strange and scary. I don't understand it at all."

"Isn't it obvious, my scaly chum? It's black magic, dark wizardry, wicked spells!" Bismark waved his stick in the air like a wand. "Trust me, *amigo*, we sugar gliders know all about the hidden forces of the forest," he added, shooting a wink at Dawn. "Yes, we are definitely doomed." Bismark scratched his scalp. "Wait *uno momento….*" He gasped. "Maybe there's no drought at all. Maybe it's evil magic, too!" His eyes bulged in horror. "Sinister sorcerers are taking our water and trying to kill us! *Mon dieu!*"

"Dawn?" Tobin asked nervously. "Do you think that's true?"

"No, I don't," she said quietly. But her thoughts were spinning. What Bismark said sounded crazy, but perhaps it wasn't far off. *It might not be "evil magic," but something has taken a hold of the forest—and whatever it is has a mission,* she thought. The fox gritted her teeth. *This drought is more than it seems.*

Dawn sighed. "We need rest." She gestured toward a small stand of trees just ahead. "We'll sleep there," she suggested, already leading the way.

Bismark scurried behind her, eager to make his bed next to hers. Tobin, however, stayed put. Although he was exhausted, he hated the idea of sleeping. Sleep would delay their mission, and Cora needed their help as quickly as possible.

But rest is necessary, Tobin told himself. *If the Brigade doesn't sleep—if we don't take care of ourselves—how can we take care of others?*

With a yawn, Tobin trudged toward the shady spot where Dawn and Bismark had stretched out, and he settled down beside them. He tried to get comfortable. He turned this way and that. He covered his eyes with his long tail. But no matter what position he took, and no matter how hard he tried to relax, his worries kept him from settling down. He couldn't stop thinking about all the frightening things that had attacked the Brigade. And when he closed his eyes, he pictured the fish and the other animals dying at the dried-out watering hole. "Dawn?" he whispered.

The fox replied only with her gentle snores.

"Bismark?" tried Tobin.

But Bismark, too, had dozed off, whistling as he slept, each of his high-pitched breaths ruffling the fur on his head.

Tobin sighed. *I have to stop thinking about this.* He knew he needed to rest and regain his strength. He closed his eyes.

For a while, the pangolin's heart kept pounding hard, and he continued to toss and turn. But, at last, his nerves calmed, his body relaxed, and he fell into a deep, deep sleep. He dreamed he was floating on his back in a cool, rushing river that carried him toward a high waterfall. As he approached the churning water, he felt a flash of fear—but it disappeared almost instantly. Because as he reached the top of the falls, he could see Cora waiting for him at the bottom. Peacefully, Tobin allowed the rushing water to carry him over the edge and into the air. And then, slowly, he floated toward the wombat—down, down, down. The pangolin reached out his arms to grab Cora's. He felt her paws—but they were not as fuzzy as he had remembered. And they were a lot smaller, too.

Tobin's eyes shot open. Bismark's face was hovering over him...and he was holding the pangolin's outstretched paws.

"You reached for me, *compadre*?" he asked.

"Oh...oh goodness," Tobin stammered. He pulled back his paws from the sugar glider's. "I was dreaming."

"Don't be ashamed, *amigo*!" Bismark laughed. "Many—dare I say most—of the valley's creatures dream of *moi.* I'm always flattered to have another admirer. I must warn you, though, I won't be returning the compliment. You see, my dreams are already occupied...by a certain someone...." Bismark turned to gaze at the still-sleeping fox...or where he thought she was sleeping. Now, there was nothing there but the mound of leaves Dawn had used as a bed.

"Oh goodness!" gasped Tobin. He sat up with a start. "Where's Dawn?"

Bismark waved a dismissive flap. "Don't worry, my fretful *amigo.* I'm sure she didn't go far. She probably just woke up early to primp and polish her coat for me." The sugar glider licked his paw then slicked back the fur on his head. "I know these are tough times, *muchacho,* but we should still try to look our best."

Tobin's eyes flickered with fear. "We need to find her," he said. "Something terrible might have happened to her."

"Relax, *compadre.* I'll find her right now. She can never resist my passionate call." Bismark cupped his paws to his mouth. "My *bella!* My lovely! My sweet! Where are you?" Bismark stood on his tiptoes and surveyed the woods for the fox. But Dawn was nowhere in sight.

"Dawn?" Tobin cried.

"*Hola*? Hello? *Mi amour*?" Bismark called out again.

But Dawn did not reply.

Bismark nervously scratched his scalp, ruffling the fur he'd just smoothed. "Hmm, maybe you're right, *muchacho*," he murmured. "Perhaps my love is in some sort of trouble."

"Oh dear," Tobin said. "What do we do?" His mind started to race. What had happened to Dawn? Suddenly, all the fears that his dream had erased came rushing back—stronger and worse than before.

Did the leaves she had slept on attack her?

Did the tree bark fly off and bite her?

Did the ground swallow her up?

Overcome with terror, Tobin started to roll into his defensive ball. But then he stopped himself. No matter how scared he was, he had to find his leader. He had to find Dawn. Suddenly, a rustle arose from the brush. "Bismark!" he gasped. "Did you hear that? Who's there?"

The sugar glider stared wide-eyed at the shrub. "It might be Dawn," he started, "or whatever took her."

Tobin swallowed hard. "We have to find out,"

he said. Summoning all his bravery, he tiptoed toward the sound.

Bismark clutched the pangolin's tail, and the animals slowly walked toward the shrubbery.

There was another rustle—louder this time.

Tobin came to an abrupt stop.

Just ahead of them, he could see the leaves tremble.

Tobin's heart raced as he approached the shaking bush and tentatively poked his snout through it. He squinted, trying to see what was making it quiver. His stomach churned. Then he saw a pair of tawny, pointed ears.

"Dawn!" he called.

"*Mi amour!*" Bismark shouted.

The animals rushed to the fox. She was unharmed. She did appear busy, though. In her mouth, she held a splintered branch that she was using to prod the ground.

"*Dios mio!* My love! You're alive!" Bismark cried, flinging himself at the fox.

"We were so worried," said Tobin, breathing a sigh of relief. "Thank goodness we found you!"

Dawn released the branch from her jaw and

propped it against a stone. "I'm sorry I scared you," she said. "I thought you'd be resting awhile longer. You were both sleeping so deeply—especially you, Tobin," she said.

The pangolin blushed as he recalled his dream about Cora.

"I left to plan our path for the night," Dawn continued. "And I came upon something interesting...."

"Hmm, yes, I see...you found a, um, 'stick' of your own." Bismark eyed Dawn's branch, puzzled. "Oh! I see what's going on!" he exclaimed, clasping his hands to his heart. "*Mon dieu,* what a beautiful gesture! You want to match me." Bismark pulled his own stick from his flap. "But you know," he continued, comparing the two, "if you want to show the world we're a couple, we *may* need to find you a more suitable stick."

"It's not the branch that's important," said Dawn. "It's what I uncovered with it." She pointed her snout to the ground where she'd cleared away some leaves and twigs. "Look!" she said.

Tobin looked down at the colored dots littering the dark ground. "Flowers?" he said.

"Yes, flowers." She beckoned her friends to come closer. "And they're not dry or dead—they're

budding…they're alive! Do you know what that means?"

Tobin and Bismark stared at her, confused.

"It means there must be water nearby," Dawn said. Her lips curled into a sly grin. "And these flowers will lead us right to it."

Chapter Twelve
RUNAWAY STICK!

Dawn lowered her head to the ground. "Snorkelworts, waterworts, spikerushes, woolyheads…."

Bismark frowned. "Pricklepanda, thorn-noggin, barb-baby! Believe me, *mon amour*, I can make up silly words, too. What are you talking about?" he cried.

Dawn sighed. "Those are the names of these flowers, Bismark." She passed her paw over them, making their petaled heads bob. "They might seem unfamiliar to you, but they're plants that grow near seasonal pools—a special type of pool that is full for only short periods of time."

Bismark crouched near a snorkelwort and touched its delicate white petals. He slid his paw down the flower's stem until it reached the ground. When he touched the dirt, his eyes lit up. "*Mon dieu!* I can practically feel the water in the roots of this snizzlewit. We're saved, *amigos!* We'll be slurping and swimming in no time!"

"We may very well be," the fox said, cautiously hopeful. "And with so many flowers here, there must surely be enough water for Cora and the entire valley."

"Oh goodness!" Tobin exclaimed.

"Now let's go," urged Dawn. "We'll follow the flowers, and they'll lead us right to the pool!"

Encouraged, Dawn and Tobin set off through the woods, trying to track the small blossoms.

Bismark, however, stood back, arms folded, watching his friends. "*Mon dieu,* all this work is not good for my image," he said. "You two look like you have the situation well under control. You clearly don't need physical assistance here. What you *do* need is my *mental* assistance." Bismark whipped out his stick and held it high in the air. "Time for me to direct this maneuver. Time for me to be maestro!" Proudly, the sugar glider waved and pointed his stick at the flowers his friends were tracking. "There's another snorkel-butt, *pangolino!* There's another fickle-fart, *mon amour!* Don't lose the trail, *mes amis!*"

"Oh... oh goodness. Thank you, Bismark," panted Tobin, continuing to hunt for the flowers.

Dawn simply shook her head.

"You're very welcome, indeed!" Oblivious to his friends' fatigue, Bismark grinned proudly, then continued to point his stick at the flowers. "We all have our special talents," he mused. "Mine happens to be giving orders. Well, *one* of mine," he corrected. "Once we succeed in finding this pool, I will demonstrate one of my *mucho* other ones. My water skills!" Bismark began to 'swim,' circling his flaps through the air.

Tobin shot a quick glance at Dawn. They both knew that Bismark could not swim a stroke. But he continued to brag. "Yes...I have much to demonstrate, *amigos.* I don't believe you've seen my belly splashes or my flap strokes. Or my death-defying spinning slip-slides and tail spins!" Bismark waved his arms grandly, twirling and whirling his stick. "And then, once I get enough speed"—he spun his stick faster and faster—"I will launch into the air and—zounds!" Bismark yelled out as his stick flew from his paw, hurtled high above him, then bounced on the ground and rolled away.

"*Mon dieu,* get back here, you rascal!" Bismark glided toward his stick, and bent to snatch it back up off the ground. But as he extended his paw, the stick skittered forward, escaping his grasp.

"What?" Bismark let out a small, confused

chuckle. "How did it do that?" Once more, he hopped after the stick and reached down to grab it—but again, it slid forward, just out of reach. "All right, enough of this slip-sliding away, *amigo,*" Bismark growled.

Determined to recapture his stick, Bismark pretended to look up at the evening sky. Casually, he whistled a tune and stroked his chin, as though he'd forgotten about the stick altogether. Then, when he was very close to it, he turned quickly and pounced on top of it. "Aha! Got you, you sticky trickster!"

But before he knew it, the stick had wriggled out from beneath him and skittered away once again! Was he seeing correctly? Bismark rubbed his eyes.

Then the sugar glider saw something else that simply couldn't possibly be. The stick seemed to be *running,* using its side segments like tiny legs!

"Hey! *Basta!* Enough!" Bismark shouted, lunging desperately after it. "This is loco, crazy, I say. Sticks don't run!"

The sugar glider picked up speed, weaving through the trees and flailing his flaps like a maniac. "There is definitely…magic…afoot!" he panted. "And I intend…to get…to the bottom of it!"

As Bismark ran after his stick, Dawn and Tobin kept clawing and pawing through the tumbleweeds, uncovering the flower path to the pool. They were so busy at work that they didn't even notice Bismark gliding and galloping into the forest, deeper and deeper, fading from view....

Chapter Thirteen
AMBUSH!

"Get back here, stick! Come to *Papi!*"

Bismark darted around trees, scurried under fallen logs, and leaped over stray tufts of tumbleweeds in desperate pursuit of his stick. But after a while, his little legs grew sore and his lungs felt short of breath.

"Come...back...I...say...." Bismark panted, slowing down to a jog. "I'm...gonna get you...." The sugar glider lowered his head and tried to catch his breath. By the time he looked up, his stick was nowhere in sight.

"*Mon dieu.*" He sighed in frustration. Then he began his search again—peering around trees, under dried leaves, and behind rocks. Bismark glanced at the night sky. Dusk had deepened to evening, and he hoped that the moon would help him find the stick. But alas, its light was too soft and dim.

"Ohhhhh, stickyyyy!" Bismark called, hoping to lure his stick with his charm. "Heeeeere, sticky, sticky! Heeeeere, stickeroo!"

Bismark walked in circles, calling for his stick. But his search was useless, and finally, he took a seat near a tree stump.

The sugar glider gazed at his surroundings and a shiver of fear ran down his tiny spine. He had been so focused on finding his stick that he hadn't watched where he was going *"Mon dieu,* I'm lost!" he said, wrapping himself in his flaps. The blackened trees here hung low,

with twisted trunks and gnarled roots. Bismark had never seen trees like these before.

"How will I ever find my way back?" Bismark wondered. He covered his face with his paws and trembled in the dark. "By all that is flappy, I'm doomed! Cooked! Conquered! Condemned—" Bismark stopped and gulped at the crackling of leaves.

"Who's there?" Quickly, the sugar glider scampered to the other side of the stump and scrunched down behind it. Then he stood back up.

"No," he declared, "I must be brave!"

He imagined Dawn, amazed by the noble tales he would tell—stories of unbelievable forest battles…of his outstanding will and wit…of his unmatched cunning and strength. "I shall not die a coward!" he bellowed. "I shall live a hero!"

Bismark took a deep breath. Then, with his flaps fully spread, he leaped out into the pale moonlight. "If there's anything lurking in this forest—any bad magic or evil spirits," he said in his boldest, most confident voice, "they better not mess with *moi*! I'm the biggest, baddest beast in the valley. I'm the strongest, scariest, most savage—"

Eeeeee!

Bismark gasped—it was the high-pitched shriek again! "Tobin?" he asked, nervously searching the shadows.

There was no answer.

"D-Dawn?" he tried.

Silence.

The sugar glider shivered. He started to tiptoe back toward the stump to hide. But then he saw something that erased all thoughts of the scary shriek. His stick had suddenly reappeared, poking up from a nearby bush.

Bismark felt his chest burn with rage. "You

runaway scoundrel, you terrible twig, you bouncing baton!" Bismark cried. "You won't escape me this time!" And without another thought, the sugar glider sprang forward and leaped at it. But just as he did...

Thwap!

A ball of tumbleweed rolled right under him, and he landed smack in the middle of it. *"Oof! Eek! Oww!"* Bismark howled. It was the biggest, prickliest, stickiest one he'd ever encountered.

"Zounds! Free me!" Bismark shouted. His arms flailed. His legs kicked out. Stalks of grass lodged in his fur. Twigs poked his eyes. "Let go of me!" he ordered. "Be gone!" But the more the sugar glider rolled and tore at the sticky tumbleweed, the deeper and deeper he sank into it.

"Release me, black magic! I command you!" The sugar glider turned and thrashed. But no matter how wildly he fought, he could not free himself. "It's suffocating me! I'm trapped!" he cried. *"Mon dieu* —this really puts the 'bush' in ambush!"

The tumbleweed tightened around Bismark, its fluff blocking his nose, masking his eyes, and clogging his ears.

"So this is what the end is like," he moaned, spitting some weeds from his mouth. "A death in fuzz!

If only I had appreciated the joys of life while I had them—the sweet taste of pomelo; Dawn's soft, luscious fur; the reflection of my handsome face in a clear pool of water. All these pleasures soon to be gone! No more! Kaput!"

In a last desperate attempt to save himself, the sugar glider released a shrill cry that echoed through the trees. *"Mon dieu! Aidez-moi!* Help!" he yelled.

When there was no answer, he screamed out again, even louder this time: "Help me! *Por favor!* HEEEEELLLLLPPPPP!!!"

But still, no one replied.

Bismark would have shouted all night—shouted until someone heard him. But before he could yell out again, the tumbleweed lodged in his throat and silenced his frantic cries.

Chapter Fourteen
THE SEARCH FOR BISMARK

"Cora will love this," said Tobin. The pangolin picked up a blossom from the forest floor and added it to the floral garland he'd made for his friend. "This necklace plus the water we find will cheer her right up."

"Yes," said Dawn, "and we must be getting close now. The flowers are more vibrant here. And the ground is moister."

The fox turned to smile at Tobin, but stopped when she heard the sound of a distant cry. Her amber eyes narrowed and her ears twitched.

"Helllppp!!!"

Tobin dropped his necklace. "Bismark?" he gulped.

"*Mon dieu! Aidez-moi!* Hellllpppp!!!"

It had to be!

The pangolin's eyes widened and frantically swept his surroundings. Brown bushes, stalks of green poking up from the moist ground, green flower buds showing hints of color to come. But no Bismark in sight. "Oh goodness, Dawn," Tobin cried. "I didn't even notice him disappear!"

Terrified, the pangolin turned to Dawn, but she had already taken off, racing toward the shouts.

"Mon dieu! Aidez-moi! Help!"

Tobin started running after the fox. But he had barely picked up speed before Dawn came to an abrupt halt. Tobin skidded to a stop behind her.

Dawn's nose twitched and her ears pivoted. "The cries have changed direction—and so fast. How is this possible?" she murmured. She lifted a paw and pointed back the opposite way. Then she set off again, retracing her steps and motioning for Tobin to follow.

"Mon dieu! Hellllllllppppppp!"

Dawn and Tobin stopped in a clearing as the voice called out again. It was Bismark, all right, but where was he? At first, the sound seemed to be ahead of them. Then it was back behind them. And now, it seemed to be coming from the right.

The animals exchanged confused glances. They raced to the right.

"*Aidez-moi!* Helllllllpppppp!!!"

Again, they skidded to a sharp stop. Now Bismark's voice was coming from the left!

Dawn and Tobin changed direction and dashed to the left. But there was no sign of Bismark anywhere!

He shouted once more. "*Mon dieu!* Helllllllpppppp! *Aidez-moi!* Helllllllpppppp!!!"

This time, the voice came from the forest. "That way," Tobin panted, pointing straight ahead, into a grove of trees. "I'm... I'm sure of it!"

Dawn nodded. Then, together, they sprinted off again into the woods.

"*Mon dieu! Aidez-moi!* Help!"

Tobin blinked. This time, the sound was coming from directly overhead. Had Bismark caught his flaps in a tree?

"Oh, no!" gasped Dawn, looking up. "It's the lyrebirds!"

Sure enough, on a twisted, low-hanging branch sat three of the long-tailed birds.

"*Mon dieu!*" sang one.

"*Aidez-moi!*" screamed another.

115

"Hellllppppp!" screeched the third.

Dawn grunted with frustration. "We can't trust what we hear," she said. "Let's try to pick up his scent."

Together, Dawn and Tobin lowered their snouts to the ground, searching for the unique mixture of woodsy musk and pomelo fruit that belonged to Bismark alone.

Sniff, sniff, sniff.

The pangolin inhaled deeply, but he could not smell anything other than the dry, burnt scent of the earth. But he did *hear* something.

Tobin tilted his ear toward the ground. Yes, there was some sort of sound—a low hum. The pangolin closed his eyes and heard it grow louder and louder. Then he started to *feel* it. The earth was vibrating! "Oh goodness!" he yelped. First a drought—and now an earthquake?

The pangolin opened his eyes. His scales shook and his stomach lurched. What he had sensed wasn't an earthquake—but it was just as frightening.

A massive tumbleweed was barreling through the forest—but this was no regular ball. This thorny orb was at least ten times the size of any that Tobin had seen, reaching the height of small trees and brutally flattening bushes as it rumbled by.

"Dawn! It's a tumbleweed! A huge one!" Tobin cried, skittering back toward the fox. "And it's coming right for us! RUN!"

Chapter Fifteen
THE HAIRY PANIC

"This way!" Dawn shouted. She and Tobin ran to the left.

The tumbleweed followed.

They dodged to the right. The tumbleweed dodged to the right.

They zigzagged through the trees—and the tumbleweed tracked them again.

The fox's heart raced. The tumbleweed was closer now. She could see that many of its pieces looked as sharp as a lion's fangs.

"Run faster!" she cried. And they did. But it was useless. The faster the animals ran, the quicker the tumbleweed barreled after them. Faster and faster it rolled, and as it caught up to them, Dawn felt its sharp barbs on her hind legs. Tobin felt its strands scratch his tail. Then the ball rolled right over them, picking the animals up, and burying them in its sticky center.

"Oof! Ow!" The pangolin winced as he was sucked deeper into the weed. Its thorns and blades wriggled between his scales, poking his tender skin. Tobin thrashed, trying to cut through the wiry grasses with his sharp claws. But quickly, he grew lightheaded and gasped, desperate for air. "I can't breathe!" The pangolin sputtered and coughed. His stomach churned with terror.

"Keep your head above the weed!" yelled the fox, who was wedged tightly in the hay next to him.

But Tobin's head was buried way down in the thick mass, and he couldn't find the strength to lift it. His stomach lurched again—and he could feel pressure building up in his rear.

He swung at the weed with his claws and tore at its spikes. But the tumbleweed seemed to fight back, pressing tighter against him, as if it were possessed by an evil spell. *Oh, goodness!* Tobin thought. *It's trying to squeeze the life out of me!*

The pangolin felt his heart sink. As the weed gripped him tighter and tighter, the pressure in his rear end grew greater and greater. He let out a low, pained grunt.

"Tobin!" called Dawn. From within the rolling ball, the fox's eyes darted left and right, struggling to spot her friend through its tangles. She caught a glimpse of his scales and could see he was still trapped in its grip.

The tumbleweed squeezed Tobin harder. One more time, he tried to lift his head. But he was too dizzy now—and a terrible panic swept through him.

Oh...oh...oh my! His stomach rumbled. The pressure in his rear grew stronger. He couldn't hold it any longer!

121

Poof! Poof! And super *POOF!*

The pangolin's scent glands finally let loose, blasting from his rear with the strength of a hurricane.

With a series of loud rips and tears, the tumbleweed exploded apart. And as chunks of weed went flying, Tobin shot upward. Curled in his protective ball, the pangolin soared high in the air, zooming up through the trees until he reached the hightest point of his flight over the treetops. For a moment, he felt himself suspended in midair. Then, suddenly, he began plummeting down, down, down, through the canopy of dry leaves, bumping and thumping through the branches until he crashed to the ground with a thud.

He groaned, dizzy and confused. Then he remembered Dawn. He sat up with a start. Where was she? Was she okay?

Tobin blinked his eyes hard, willing himself to see clearly. Then he rose to his feet and turned toward the terrible ball of tumbleweed. But when he saw it, it was no longer moving—and it was no longer really a ball.

"Oh goodness!" said Tobin. His blast had blown the tumbleweed out in every direction, leaving clumps scattered throughout the forest. And the biggest part—the one that remained in one piece—was more like a pancake now than a ball—flattened and lifeless, weighed down by the oily substance that had shot from his glands.

If the tumbleweed had been under an evil spell, it was clear that it no longer was. Tobin's foul-smelling spray had blasted its power away.

"Dawn!" Tobin called out, searching for the fox. He pawed nervously through damp lumps of weed. Then he spotted her a few trees away. The fox shook off the weed that clung to her fur and pushed herself to her feet.

"Oh goodness, I'm so glad you're okay!" said the pangolin.

"I'm glad you're all right, too," said Dawn.

The two friends stared at the tufts of tumbleweed scattered before them and caught their breath in silence. The threat was gone, and everything had turned quiet. Not a single leaf rustled; not the slightest breeze blew.

And then the stillness was broken.

"Way to go, *pangolino!*"

"Bismark!" Dawn and Tobin cried out.

The sugar glider emerged from behind a bush, his stick clasped firmly in hand. "You fought the weed and won, scaly chum! But really, did you have to spray me, too?"

"Oh goodness—I didn't know you were here!" said Tobin.

"*Mais oui!* I was stuck in the ball right beside you!" Bismark exclaimed. "Didn't you feel my magnificent presence?" The sugar glider sniffed his arm and wrinkled his nose. "*Mon dieu!* That stench, that odor, that tang! This calls for the flaps!" Bismark extended his arms, then he pumped his flaps up and down, airing them out.

The pangolin bowed his head in embarrassment. "Sorry, Bismark."

A wide grin crossed Bismark's face. "No matter, *muchacho!*" he said, throwing an arm around Tobin. "You may have poofed my pelt, but it was for a very good cause. You saved us all from that hairy panic!"

Chapter Sixteen
REUNITED

"Oh, *mon amour,* milady, my love—how our separation pained me!" The sugar glider ran toward Dawn, embraced her leg in his flaps, and buried his face in her fur. "I will never abandon you again, fair fox! Especially not after you dove into that terrible tumbleweed just to save your one true love!"

Dawn rolled her eyes and gently shook off the glider, though she could not help but grin.

"Oh goodness, we're happy you're safe," said the pangolin. "But Bismark...what happened to you? Where did you go?"

"This stick came alive, *amigo!*" he cried, waving it in the air. "It led me astray, I tell you. It lured me right into the clutches of its hairy comrade—the tumbleweed!" He pointed to some of the scattered pieces. Then he furrowed his brow at his stick and planted it in the ground with a scowl. "This forest is under some kind of spell! We need to leave pronto, before this all goes too far. We must find a new home! New forests! New gliding grounds!"

"Oh goodness." Tobin gulped. He could not bear the thought of leaving the valley. It was his home. But then he thought about their narrow escape from the tumbleweed and all that had happened. "Maybe Bismark is right," he whispered. His body started to tremble. "Maybe we should flee the forest now before it's too late."

Dawn placed a comforting paw on Tobin's shoulder. "We are not leaving our valley. We are going to find water," she said. "We are the Nocturnal Brigade, and we will not give up our home or our mission."

Tobin nodded, but still, his scales shook with fear. "It's j-just..." he began nervously, "h-how will we ever find water without the forest destroying us?"

"*Si*, yes, good question, *amigo*," said Bismark. "But more importantly: how will I ever get all this tumbleweed out of my fur?" The sugar glider brushed bits of grass and sticks from his fur then, scrunching his nose with displeasure, he plucked a strand from his ear.

Suddenly, Dawn's amber eyes lit up with the spark of a new idea. "That's it!" she cried. "Bismark,

126

leave those weeds in your fur. In fact, put more on."
Dawn picked up a clump of tumbleweed and placed it
on Bismark's head.

"Pah!" Bismark's entire small body convulsed
with disgust. He whipped himself back and forth until
the tumbleweed flew to the ground. *Mon dieu!* I adore
you, my darling, but have you lost your beautiful mind?"

Dawn grinned. "No, Bismark. This is how we'll
avoid the forest dangers. We'll cover ourselves in the
weed for camouflage!"

Bismark's mouth dropped open. *"Mon amour, mi
bella,* my sweet...forgive me for saying so, but that plan
is *absolument terrible!* You say you want to *avoid* the
forest dangers?" He pointed at a clump of tumbleweed.
"That is the forest danger! At least, it's one of them."

"Oh goodness, he's right," Tobin agreed, backing
away from the weeds. "The tumbleweeds just attacked
us. What if they do it again?"

Dawn sighed. "It's a risk," she admitted. "But it's
one we have to take." The fox picked up a small clump of
tumbleweed. "I'll put some on first to test it."

Bismark and Tobin watched nervously as the
fox placed the weeds on her back. Then they stared at it,
wondering if it would strike. But after several moments,
the weed remained motionless and limp on Dawn's fur.

"*Mon dieu!*" Bismark looked at Tobin, impressed. "You really knocked that weed ball out cold!"

The pangolin smiled bashfully. "I...I suppose it's safe now," he said.

"*Si.* But there's another *problemo,*" said Bismark. The sugar glider examined the fur on his arms and legs. Then he craned his neck to inspect his back. "I know my pelt isn't quite as perfect as usual, but still—*por favor,* please admit—my hide is far too exquisite to hide!"

Dawn ignored him. She picked up a big clump of tumbleweed and tossed it toward her friend.

"The things I do for that lady fox." Bismark sighed. Then, reluctantly, using only the tip of a single paw, he picked up a strand of the weed and set it right on his bald spot.

Tobin, though, did not move. Even undercover, traveling would be dangerous. What if their disguises were detected? He wasn't sure he could survive another tumbleweed attack.

But then he thought of Cora. His heart ached as he imagined her—dehydrated, scared, and alone. She needed water. She needed *him.* Tobin dug his claws in the dirt, gathering his courage. Any plan, no matter how risky, was worth trying if it might save Cora's life.

With a deep, steadying breath, Tobin slowed his

racing pulse. Then, he began to collect the tumbleweed, wrapping it around his body and tucking it into his scales.

But even as he did—even with Cora in mind—his stomach lurched with fear. Would this disguise really work? Or would the forest's black magic see right through it?

Chapter Seventeen
UNDERCOVER

"*Voilà!*" Bismark cried out, waving his stick grandly. "How do I look?"

Dawn and Tobin stared at the sugar glider. He'd fashioned the tumbleweed around himself so that he resembled some sort of bird.

"Are...are you supposed to be a duck?" Tobin asked.

Bismark scowled. "Of course not! Don't I look like a proud peacock? Or a fearsome falcon taking his last flight just before sunset?"

"You look like a sugar glider with a little bit of tumbleweed stuck to him," Dawn said. She lifted more tumbleweed from the ground with her jaws and packed it around Bismark's neck. Then she added some to his hindquarters. "You need to be disguised," she told him. "That means anyone who sees you should believe you are just a ball of tumbleweed rolling through."

Bismark let out a loud, disgruntled humph. "Someone as handsome as *moi* should not be hidden like this. Get this off of me, I say," he demanded through a layer of weeds. "Remove it at once!" Bismark's protests continued, but his voice grew fainter and fainter as Dawn covered him with more and more tumbleweed.

"Oh goodness." Tobin sighed. Just moments ago, he worried that the tumbleweed would smother him again, but now, he couldn't even keep it on. The pangolin was trembling so much that as soon as he placed a clump on his scales, it slipped right off. *This won't fool anyone,* he fretted. *What were we thinking?* Camouflage had seemed like a good idea at first, but now it seemed completely useless. As Tobin's nerves mounted, his scales shook even harder, shedding every last bit of tumbleweed.

Dawn placed a comforting paw on one of Tobin's. Then, using her snout, she lifted a clump of weeds and placed it on her friend's back, ensuring it was firmly tucked in his scales.

"This will work, Tobin," she said, looking directly into his eyes.

A hint of fear flickered across the pangolin's face, but he nodded, showing his trust

132

in his leader. Dawn continued to pack tumbleweed onto Tobin's scales until they were completely covered. When she was finished, all that could be seen of the pangolin were his claws and the tip of his tail.

After ensuring her disguise thoroughly covered her, the fox studied her friends. They were unrecognizable. They were ready to take on the forest. *But would this really work?* she wondered. *If there really was something out there, could a simple disguise outsmart it?*

The fox cleared her throat. "Let's go," she commanded, pressing on into the woods. She had to dismiss her worries. This was the only way they might succeed. "We have to follow the flowers to find the pool." Dawn gazed down through the gaps in her tumbleweed at the blooming blossoms below. Then she set off, following their colorful path.

Slowly and clumsily, the animals traveled through the forest in three blobs of descending size order—Dawn, the largest and longest, was first. Tobin, medium-sized and oblong, was second. And Bismark, the tiniest and also the loudest, was third. Annoyed grunts and shrill shouts rang without stop from the sugar glider's tangle of weeds.

"My flaps are covered in goop!

"My beautiful brown eyes cannot see!

"My body tingles and tickles…and not in a good way!"

"Bismark," hissed Dawn.

But the sugar glider would not cease his rant.

"There's grass in my ear!

"There's a weed in my nose!

"There's a stick in my you-know-what!"

"HOLD IT RIGHT THERE!" An unfamiliar voice boomed through the forest, finally silencing Bismark's complaints.

The trio froze, startled and terrified. They'd been spotted! Someone knew they were hidden in the tumbleweeds! But who was it? The animals anxiously looked all around. There was no one in sight.

"HOLD IT RIGHT THERE!" The voice came again.

"Who said that?" yelled Bismark, calling back at the voice.

"Shhh," Dawn warned Bismark.

"Whoever it is...d-don't make him angry," Tobin whispered.

"HOLD IT RIGHT THERE!" Once more, the menacing command boomed through the trees.

"*Mon dieu!* Enough! We're holding it!" Bismark cried. "What do you want, already?"

"We're holding it! What do you want, already?" Bismark's voice echoed again through the forest, but this time, it wasn't coming from him.

Dawn gazed up, following the sound of the voice. Her eyes narrowed. There, just overhead, perched atop a low branch—lyrebirds! Again!

"*Dios mio!* You've got to be kidding me!" Bismark grumbled. "Those birdbrains frustrate my flaps!"

Dawn sighed, echoing Bismark's annoyance.

135

Tobin, though, felt relieved. "At least it's just the lyrebirds," he said. "I thought something was out there to get us!"

The fox nodded. "Let's keep going," she said.

Dawn set off again, leading the pack and following the trail of flowers. *What a startling false alarm,* she thought, glancing back at the pesky birds. She wished they would just fly away or go to sleep for the night instead of scaring them at every turn. *What a dull life it must be to repeat what's heard. Never stating an original thought—just dumbly mimicking others.*

Dawn stopped. *Mimicking others.* Where had the lyrebirds heard someone shouting, "HOLD IT RIGHT THERE!" They must have heard it somewhere. All they did was repeat. But who had said it, and why?

It was a puzzle Dawn wanted to solve, but there was no time. Her thoughts were interrupted by Bismark's shout up ahead.

"We found it!" he cried. The sugar glider jumped up and down in his tumbleweed ball and let out a happy whoop. "Water, *mes amis!* We found water!"

Chapter Eighteen
THE FLOATING TONGUE

Standing beside the pool's banks, the trio looked at the water in awe. It was unlike anything they had ever seen. It didn't just shimmer in the moonlight—it *glowed*...with a whole rainbow of rich and radiant colors. Brilliant blues, vibrant greens, and vivid pinks gleamed from its depths, lighting the pool from within.

Tobin was amazed, but the water also frightened him. He took a step backward into the brush. Were their minds playing tricks on them again? Were these colors real? Or were they the work of more evil magic?

"The algae living in this water create the colors," Dawn whispered, easing the pangolin's fear. "It's nothing to be scared of."

"Nothing to be scared of, indeed!" agreed Bismark. "It's miraculous, magnificent, *maravilloso!* In fact, it's perfect for my fountain!" The sugar glider

popped his head up from his tumbleweed to fully take in the sight. "You know, I originally imagined gemstones to mark my statue's fabulous facial features," he said. "But, *mon dieu!* With this colorful stuff spouting from it, the entire *body* will sparkle!"

"The water *is* beautiful," Tobin agreed. Now that Dawn had helped calm his nerves, the pangolin could truly appreciate the glittering sight before him. His eyes widened, dazzled by the band of colors dancing along the pool's surface. "And it's big, too," he added.

"Yes," Dawn agreed with a grin. "There's enough water here to last the valley the entire dry season."

The trio sighed with relief. They had finally found water. Now, all they had left to do was bring Cora to it and alert the other sick animals.

Tobin smiled. Everything would be all right.

"HOLD IT RIGHT THERE!"

The trio jumped. That harsh voice—it was back!

"Probably those pesky lyres again," Bismark reasoned.

But when the animals surveyed the banks, there were no birds in sight.

Dawn's fur stood on end, and Tobin began to tremble. Bismark's eyes darted nervously from one friend to the other.

"HOLD IT RIGHT THERE!"

There it was again.

Tobin looked at the glowing pool. "Oh goodness—what's that?" he gasped, raising a trembling paw.

On the pool's far bank was another chute similar to the one they'd seen at the watering hole. It was the length of a tree trunk, and it was moving toward the pool. But this one was extra strange. It was hovering in the air!

"HOLD IT RIGHT THERE!"

Immediately, the floating chute halted.

"It's obeying the mystery voice!" Tobin said.

"A magic chute obeying a magical voice. But of course!" Bismark sputtered. "It's black magic, I tell you. Sorcery has overtaken it!"

"I don't believe in magic," Dawn replied. Her voice came out steady and certain—but she was beginning to doubt herself. As hard as she tried, she could not muster any logical explanation for what she saw.

"NOW SPILL IT!"

The three friends watched, eyes wide, jaws dropping, as the chute obeyed the mystery speaker's command. It tilted up at its back end—and a stream of water poured out of it, splashing into the pool.

How can that chute float in the air like that?

Dawn wondered, working the question over in her mind.

"HA-HA-HA-HA!" The voice laughed triumphantly.

Again, the Nocturnal Brigade turned in a circle, searching in every direction, trying to locate the source of the strange commands. But still, they saw no one.

"Come!" it rang out again. "The water is ours! The great unveiling is near! It is time for our celebration!"

Then, just as before by the watering hole, the chute blasted apart into hundreds of tiny fragments. A flurry of leaves, twigs, and bark bits scattered through the air.

"I knew it!" Bismark remarked in a shrill whisper. "The plants are under a spell and are working against us. They're all in cahoots!"

Suddenly, a hot wind swept through the clearing, rippling the pool's rainbow waters and rustling the plants on the banks.

"Oh goodness—look!" Tobin gasped.

The friends watched a large lily pad float from the edge of the pool. When it finally reached the center, the full midnight moon overhead shone down upon it.

The trio could not help but draw in their breath.

Standing on the lily pad was the most unusual creature they had ever seen.

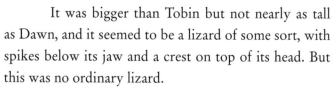

It was bigger than Tobin but not nearly as tall as Dawn, and it seemed to be a lizard of some sort, with spikes below its jaw and a crest on top of its head. But this was no ordinary lizard.

Tobin flinched as the creature jumped onto its back legs and spread its arms wide, revealing a staff in his claw.

"*Mon dieu!*" Bismark whispered, aghast. "This sorcerer has a scepter…just like mine!"

The creature raised his stick high in the air like a wand, and vivid colors swept across his body. At first, he appeared to be shades of blue—navy, then sapphire, then teal. But those blues quickly shifted to greens—dark, medium, then light—then changed again, to bright yellow. Next, with a faint *click*, the creature disappeared altogether…until it magically reappeared on another broad lily pad closer to shore. And then another one farther away!

The Brigade watched, awestruck, as the mysterious magician continued to disappear and reappear, changing color all the while.

"*Dios mio!* What mad hocus-pocus is this?" Bismark shrieked. "He's here, then there, then back again…. Before we know it, he'll be popping up right in front of my beautiful face!"

But when the creature did appear again, he was back in the center of the pool. Perched on his lily pad, he paused then turned, as if he were surveying his magic domain.

His eyes flickered over the water in the strangest way—one looked left while the other looked right at the very same time. Thoughtfully, he stroked the beard under his chin and lowered his stick to his side. And then—click! Without warning, he vanished again.

Dawn, Tobin, and Bismark stared at the pool in stunned silence. Then the sugar glider let out a yelp. "It's a demon!" he cried.

"Oh Dawn, we—we have to run!" Tobin stammered. He stepped back from the pond, but he stopped at a new strange sight before him.

An incredibly long, purplish tongue suddenly appeared over the pool. A floating tongue—a tongue with no body, attached to nothing but air. With a lightning-fast flick, it unfurled and began to lap at the colorful water. Slurping sounds filled the clearing and glowing droplets splashed in all directions, glimmering like gems in the moonlight.

"Wait a moment...."
The fox narrowed her

amber eyes. Then, suddenly, they widened. "That's no demon we just saw!" she said. "That tongue explains everything!"

"A tongue with no body?" Bismark raised his brows. "How does that explain *anything?*"

"We don't see the body," Dawn explained, "but that doesn't mean it's not there. It's just 'invisible'—camouflaged—changing colors to blend in with its background." The fox looked at her friends. "This creature is not a demon. It's a chameleon!"

"*Mon dieu!*" Bismark said. "A piddly little lizard with powerful magic!"

"No, that's just it, Bismark." Dawn shook her head "This isn't magic. None of it has been." Her face brightened. "All the strange things in the forest that we couldn't explain...I think I can explain them now...."

Chapter Nineteen
THE VEILED CREATURES

"I can't believe we didn't realize it sooner," Dawn murmured, still shaking her head in awe.

"Realize what?" asked the pangolin.

"All the things in the forest we thought were 'coming alive' were alive all along," said Dawn.

Tobin tilted his head in confusion.

The fox faced her friends. "Think of the way bugs look," she said.

"Icky? Nasty? Disgusting?" Bismark wrinkled his nose and spat. "No offense, *mon amour,* but I have a better brain exercise—thinking of *beautiful* creatures. Like you and me!"

"No, Bismark. Think about their sizes, their colors, their shapes. Take a grasshopper, for example. How would you describe it?"

"Hmm," mused the sugar glider. "A skinny little

insect that's much less attractive than *moi*?"

"It's long, thin, and green," answered Tobin.

"Yes," said Dawn. "Like—"

"—like grass!" Tobin finished.

"That's right," said the fox. "Grasshoppers blend in with their surroundings. Their appearance is like a disguise that protects them from threatening predators."

Tobin thought about the other bugs he had seen crawling near his burrow. "What about caterpillars?" he asked. "They're green and fuzzy, like moss. They can blend in with their surroundings, too."

"Yes." Dawn nodded. "And there are bugs that look like tree bark or plants or flowers. There's a thorn bug that looks just like thorns on a plant. And a dead-leaf butterfly that looks like a brown, withered leaf."

"I've never seen *those* bugs," said Tobin.

"Neither have I," Bismark added.

"That's the point," said Dawn. "They are there, but you don't see them. They are hidden in plain sight." The fox started to pace near the reeds. "It all makes sense now. The swirling earth we saw wasn't quicksand—it was hundreds of sandy grasshoppers. And the tree bark that attacked you?" Dawn looked at Bismark. "It wasn't tree bark at all—it was bark bugs."

"What about the chutes?" Tobin asked.

"They're made of insects, too—leaf bugs and stick bugs tightly clustered together," Dawn explained.

"*Mon dieu!*" Bismark exclaimed. "All this time, we were tricked and tortured by insects!"

"It's not just insects that disguise themselves," said Dawn. She pointed to the chameleon, who had reappeared on a mossy stone near the bank. "There are reptiles who can change color to match their surroundings, too."

Tobin squinted at the chameleon, who was now a rich shade of green. "That's amazing," he said. "All these creatures were hiding...just like we did in the tumbleweed!"

"Incredible, unbelievable, inconceivable!" Bismark ranted, frowning over his tumbleweed torso. "We used camouflage to hide from the camouflagers!"

"Exactly." Dawn smiled. But the calm that came with her new understanding quickly faded. "I still don't know though.... Why are these creatures hoarding water in the middle of a drought? Why are they attacking us? Why have they turned against the other animals?"

"It's treachery!" Bismark declared, pointing his stick in the air. "Treachery most foul! And I, for one, am going to put a stop to it."

Bismark shook his limbs free of their tumbleweed

cover. Then he sauntered toward the chameleon, swinging his arms in a carefree stroll. He wasn't a bit afraid. "Bugs and a little lizard?" He laughed. "No *problemo* at all for a sugar glider."

"Bismark!" Dawn cried out.

"Come back!" pleaded the pangolin.

But Bismark pressed on, unworried "Please, *mes amis*, have no fear. With my massive muscles, I could flap these guys silly."

"No!" Dawn called out again. "There's a lot we don't know, Bismark. That chameleon is not just a little lizard...he could be dangerous!" Determined to stop her foolish friend, the fox leaped after him, but the sugar glider was already far beyond reach, marching out into the clearing. He chuckled and tossed the last of his tumbleweed disguise to the ground—and a group of insects scurried out of it.

The sugar glider crouched low to take a closer look at the bugs. "*Mon dieu!*" he exclaimed. "Now I understand! You little buggies were hidden inside the tumbleweed, steering and guiding it. That's how it could follow us. And shove us, and snag us, and snatch us!" Bismark chuckled. "No wonder the weed seemed alive. It was!"

Bismark saw a bright green leaf flutter by. "Ah ha!" he declared, pointing his stick at the creature. "My stunning peepers are fooled no more. You're not a leaf. You're a leaf bug!" He gave a satisfied nod. "And you!" he continued, looking down at a brown patch of tree bark. "You're a bark bug." Bismark nudged the insect with his stick until it crawled out of reach.

"AHEM!"

Bismark looked up. The chameleon, still perched on his rock, was staring down at him.

When Bismark met his gaze, the chameleon's yellow face changed to orange, then angry red. Then it faded into a mellow pink as his lips curled into a sinister smile.

"Who is this little rodent?" the chameleon jeered at the sugar glider.

"What rodent?" asked Bismark, gazing around him then abandoning his search with a shrug.

"Do you know who you have the honor of standing before?" the chameleon bellowed.

Bismark put his hands on his hips. "A crazy little lizard?"

The chameleon snorted at the insult and puffed out his chest. "I am King Kami, Ruler of All Veiled Creatures," he announced proudly, raising his stick. He swept his other arm out. "And this is my Insect Army."

"Yes, we've met," Bismark said, rolling his eyes. "But you can stop this whole show. Bismark—macho marsupial, fearless warrior, and sugar glider *extraordinaire*—has no fear of a bunch of little bugs and a puny chameleon."

"A puny chameleon, hmm?" Standing tall, King Kami waved his wand overhead. "Come, my Insect Army," he boomed, his eyes flickering a feverish yellow. "Let's show our visitor what we do to unwelcome guests."

Chapter Twenty
BISMARK'S WATERY DOOM

King Kami's scales blazed a deep, fiery red. He craned his neck forward. Then, before Bismark could even blink, he unleashed his long, purple tongue and whipped it around the sugar glider, wrapping him tightly.

"Unleash me, you vile fiend! Unhand me, you despicable beast! Un-tongue me, you unsanitary assailant!" Bismark squirmed and flexed his flaps, trying to glide free, but the chameleon's tongue held strong.

"Let me go! Let me go!" Bismark howled. But the more he complained, the tighter the tongue gripped him, crushing his flaps to his sides and squeezing the air from his lungs.

"Oh goodness, we have to help him!" cried Tobin. The pangolin moved through the brush toward his friend, but his tumbleweed covering slowed him down.

"We need to move fast!" Dawn whispered, shaking the weeds off her back. "Take off your disguise... but stay hidden."

Dawn and Tobin crept forward, dodging the beam of the full moon and the glow of the pool's colored lights. They kept to the shadows as they made their way toward the struggling Bismark.

"Help!" shrieked the sugar glider, writhing and twisting in vain. "Helllllllpppp!" Flicking his tiny wrist, Bismark used his stick to bat at the tongue. With his other hand, he pulled at it, trying to stretch it and loosen its hold. When neither of those worked, he resorted to desperate measures—he craned his neck toward the tongue. Then, scrunching his nose in disgust...*chomp!* He clamped his teeth down on it.

But King Kami didn't flinch.

Bismark's efforts had no effect at all—except to anger his captor more.

Pyah! Pyeu! Puh! Bismark spat out the chameleon's saliva and then—*huuuuuuuuuhhhh!*—he struggled to take in a breath as the chameleon's grip grew even tighter.

And then, with a sharp jolt, the chameleon extended his tongue and dangled the sugar glider out over the pool.

"Nooooo!" Bismark screamed. This was no puddle—this pool was deep! And despite his earlier boasting, Bismark could not swim at all.

Slowly, tauntingly, the chameleon lowered him over the shimmering surface.

Bismark's heart pounded as the water drew closer.

"Oh goodness...Dawn!" Tobin froze in the brush. "The chameleon is going to drop him! Bismark—" the pangolin gulped, struggling to say the horrible words, "—Bismark is going to drown!"

The fox's thoughts started to race. How could they save him? She stared hard at her friend flailing helplessly. Think. Think. The fox gritted her teeth, determined. Her amber eyes flashed as a plan formed in her mind.

"This way," she said. Taking care to move quietly, the fox raced toward the chameleon.

She and Tobin were good swimmers, she reasoned. If they could sneak up behind King Kami and catch him off guard, perhaps they could save the sugar glider. It was a good plan, but they'd have to run halfway around the pool—a great distance—to reach the chameleon. Her chest tightened with worry. If they did not get there quickly, then Bismark had no hope at all.

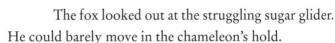

The fox looked out at the struggling sugar glider. He could barely move in the chameleon's hold.

"*Oh, mon dieu*—this is it! The end! The finale! *La fin!*" Bismark wailed. He gazed longingly at the shore. "So long, sweet earth! Farewell, stinky friend! *Au revoir*, one true love!"

King Kami lowered Bismark so his feet were touching the water.

"*Dios mio*," moaned Bismark. He hung his head in defeat. "The only good thing in all this is that my coat will be clean when I die."

Eeeeee!

The sugar glider jerked his head up at the sound of a sharp noise beneath him. "What was that?" he cried. He anxiously eyed the water.

EEEEEE!

There it was again! But louder this time—more insistent. Bismark's eyes bulged. Was there some sort of creature in the pool? Was something going to attack him from below?

Bismark started to kick his tiny legs, hoping to keep the creature away. "*Mon dieu!*" he blubbered. "An evil lizard up here and a mysterious creature down below? How could this get any worse? I'm doomed!"

EEEEEE!

Bismark gasped. Another scream! But now he could hear it more clearly.

The sugar glider furrowed his brow. This was no creature from below. He recognized this noise. It was a high-pitched shriek—the same one he had heard earlier in the forest. The sound he had accused Tobin of making. But now, he was sure…it was coming from his paw. The sugar glider gaped at his stick. Could it be?

Eeee ooo eee iii ooo ahh!

"Dios mio!" That sounded like more than a shriek, Bismark thought. *It sounded like…words.* He gulped. Was his stick *speaking?* With a flick of his wrist, the sugar glider angled the stick so its tip was close to his ear.

"Oh *mon dieu!*" he marveled.

Back in the forest, Bismark couldn't hear the sound clearly because it was so high-pitched and faint. But now—surrounded by nothing but water, with no other noises around him—he was certain. That shrill scream was a voice!

Bismark blinked hard in amazement. Yes, his stick was speaking! It was alive!

"Of course…." he began, putting the pieces together. His stick was no stick at all. It was a bug! A bug that *looked* like a stick!

For a moment, Bismark stared, dumbfounded. Then his face twisted in anger. "How could you do this to me? Deceive me, trick me, bamboozle me!" Bismark glowered at the stick bug. "You lured me into the forest and into a trap. You led me right into that terrible tumbleweed so it could capture me!" He shook his head. "After all I've done for you—keeping you close to my beautiful side, making you my scepter of power, praising you left and—*noooo!*"

The sugar glider screeched as King Kami lowered him further into the pool. Now, the water was up to his waist. Furious and fearful, he opened his mouth to yell at his evil captor. But before he could utter a word—

"Wait!" The stick bug twisted and let out a desperate squeal. "King Kami, if you drown the squirrel, you'll drown me, too!" His words came out strong and clear.

The sugar glider's face burned with fury. "I am not a—!" He stopped himself short. "*Uno momento,* sticky," he mused. "That chameleon may be crazy, but he wouldn't drown a member of his own insect army. You're the key to my rescue!" Bismark grinned then called out to the reptile. "Yoo-hoo! *Hola,* King Cuckoo?"

The chameleon met Bismark's gaze.

"It's time for you to stop this whole drown-the-glider game. I've got one of your friends—and I'm not letting him go!" Bismark flicked his wrist side to side, flaunting the stick bug in his paw.

King Kami let out a grunt, and his eyes blazed a fiery orange.

"Yes, si, it's true. Game over, *compadre*," smirked Bismark. "You might as well reel me in now. Ha, ha, ha!" The sugar glider let out a satisfied laugh. "Once again, I am victorious. No one defeats *this* marsupial!"

But King Kami did not reel Bismark in. Instead, the chameleon hurled back his arm and launched his sceptor high in the air. It glistened in the moonlight as it turned end over end—and then suddenly sprouted wings!

"*Dios mio!*" cried Bismark, his bulbous eyes tracing the flight. King Kami's "magic wand" wasn't magic at all. In fact, it wasn't even a wand. It was a stick bug, too—a flying stick bug!

As the insect zipped through the sky, Bismark grew tense. If that stick bug could fly, he wondered, what else could it do?

With a flutter of its thin wings, the flying bug hovered in front of the sugar glider. And then—*zoom!*— the insect shot right at him and landed on Bismark's clenched fist.

"Arrrrghhhh!" Bismark shuddered and shrieked. "Get off me, you wicked wing-thing! Fly away, you sticky swooper!"

"*Eeeeee!* Help me!" cried Bismark's stick bug.

With two twig-like hands, the flying stick bug grabbed his friend and pulled, gathering force from his leaf-like wings.

But Bismark held tightly to his bug. "Sorry, *amigo,*" he said, clenching his fist even harder around him, "but you're the only reason I'm alive. I'm not letting you go!"

But as Bismark strengthened his grip, so did King Kami, coiling his long, purple tongue tighter and tighter around Bismark's gut. The sugar glider thrashed, trying to free his arms and legs. But the more he struggled, the harder King Kami squeezed. Slowly, Bismark grew weaker. His limbs were tingling and his body was turning numb. He couldn't hold on any longer.

The sugar glider yelped in despair as his fingers fell limp and the stick bug went free. Bismark watched, helpless, as the flying stick bug carried his friend to safety.

"Wait!" Bismark cried, calling after the insects. "Please, *por favor!* Save me, too!" But the stick bugs did not return.

158

The sugar glider grew dizzy as he realized that there was nothing protecting him now. "Hellllppp!" he screamed one last time.

But it was too late.

King Kami's eyes turned a blazing shade of gold. Then, he unraveled his tongue, dropped Bismark into the pool, and watched with glee as the sugar glider's head disappeared under the shimmering water.

Chapter Twenty-One
THE BATTLE OF THE HIDDEN KINGDOM

"Oh, goodness! Noooo!" Tobin wailed.

He and Dawn had raced as fast as they could to reach the chameleon, but they were only halfway there when the creature let Bismark go.

Tobin and Dawn froze in shock. They stared at the place where Bismark had sunk. For a moment, the water was still, and all they could see was its smooth surface and its colorful glow.

Then—*splash!*

Bismark's flaps broke the pool's surface. Struggling for air, the sugar glider's face emerged, ragged and drenched.

"Hurry!" Dawn took off toward the bank closest to Bismark. "We have to jump in and save him!"

"Help! Help!" Bismark sputtered.

King Kami stared coldly at the struggling sugar glider. Then he turned to address his army. "It is time for the great unveiling!" he boomed. "It is time for the Hidden Kingdom to rise!"

At the sound of the king's command, the clearing began to buzz. The ground fluttered and pulsed. The trees trembled and shook. Then, all at once, millions of veiled creatures—bugs that looked like leaves, thorns, vines, sticks, and sand—leaped from their places of hiding and swirled into a giant, funnel-shaped swarm.

Eeeeeee! Eeeeeee!

"Save me!" yelped Bismark, spitting out mouthfuls of water. "Helllllpppp!"

"Oh goodness, we're coming!" yelled Tobin. His words rang out through the clearing—and gave him and Dawn away.

The pangolin gasped and clasped his paws to his mouth. "Oh no! I'm sorry, Dawn!"

The fox yanked her friend down into the grass. But it was too late. King Kami's eyes darted in separate directions, then both locked right on them. The chameleon cackled. Then, with a sweep of an arm, he signaled his army. "Stop them!" he commanded.

At once, the insect funnel changed shape. The

insects spread out, forming a wide, pulsing wall and completely blocked the pool.

"Oh no!" Tobin gasped. "What do we do? How do we get to Bismark?"

Dawn struggled to catch sight of her friend. But the insect wall was too dense. She could not see the pool at all. She could only hear Bismark's screams.

"*Mon dieu!* Help me! I'm drowning!" he shrieked.

Dawn and Tobin searched frantically, looking for a gap in the wall to run through, but it was solid. And it only continued to thicken and rise as more and more insects joined to build it.

"We have to break through it," the fox whispered. "We have no other choice."

Tobin's scales started to shudder, but he knew that's what they had to do.

Together, the two friends barreled toward the giant bug barrier.

"Hold on, Bismark!" yelled Dawn.

"We're coming!" cried Tobin.

But there was no reply.

Dawn's breath caught in her throat. Tobin felt a sharp pang in his side. Were they too late? The fox shook

her head, forcing the terrible thought from her mind—
and she ran harder, charging right into the pulsing wall
of insects.

The bugs attacked in a giant swarm. They stung
and scratched every part of her body. They bit her snout
and dove into her eyes.

Tobin could barely see through the thick cloud
of insects. They surrounded him, trying to bite and sting
him. His armored scales shielded his skin, but Dawn

was completely exposed. Her fur was not thick enough to protect her, and her skin burned and itched under the insects' attack. Frantically, she batted at the bugs, swiping them away. But they were overpowering her, and her body began to swell.

"I have to help her!" cried Tobin. He swiped the air with his claws, forcing the bugs to scatter. Then, whipping his tail from side to side, he cleared a path for Dawn so she could head to the pool. "Run!" he cried out to her.

But as soon as Dawn lunged down the path, King Kami let out a furious howl. With a sudden *flick,* he released his tongue, aiming right for the fox's throat.

The pangolin's eyes widened in horror as the long, purple rope shot through the air like a lightning bolt. "No, you don't!" Tobin yelled. Then—*whoosh!*— he shot out his own powerful tongue. Soaring at full speed, the pangolin's pink tongue stopped the chameleon's purple one, whacking it sideways and batting it away from the fox.

"Dawn! Huwwy!" urged Tobin. His tongue was still pressed against King Kami's.

Dawn raced to the pool, heart pounding, jaw clenched. *I'm too late,* she thought, a lump forming deep in her throat. There was no way Bismark could have stayed afloat for this long. Surely he had sunk in the water, struggled to breathe, and drowned.

But when the fox arrived at the pond's bank, there was Bismark, alive and well, standing on a lily pad, legs wide, knees bent, and fists poised in a boxing position.

Dawn exhaled a huge sigh of relief.

"Bring it on, buggies!" shouted the sugar glider, bracing himself for a fight. "*En garde,* insects!"

The swarm rose into the air. Then, moving as a single cloud, they turned in Bismark's direction.

Bismark raised his fists higher. He was ready for their attack. "A bunch of bugs can't scare *moi!*" You don't know who you're up against!" he shouted. "I'm Battling Bismark! Victor of the Valley! The Gliding Gladiator! The Bug Blaster!!!"

Bismark's eyes blazed with confidence, but as he watched the insects his pupils widened and gleamed with fear. The swarm of bugs was now forming a new shape: a battering ram.

Whop!

Moving in unison, the beam of bugs bonked Bismark over the head.

"Ouch!" Bismark yelped, raising his paws to his bald spot. "Shoo! Scram! Get off of me, I say!"

But the bugs continued the battle, nipping, stinging, and scratching the sugar glider on every part of his tiny body.

Dawn clenched her jaw and her spine arched with fury. Then, without hesitation, she crouched and sprung off the bank into the depths of the pool. "I'm coming, Bismark!" she shouted, quickly paddling toward him.

"Oh, my *bella,* my sweet!" Bismark cried gratefully. "You've come to save your beloved!" Though the bugs still bit at his skin, the sugar glider sighed with relief.

The fox swam faster, pumping her paws at full speed. Now, she was just a few strokes away from her friend. "Bismark!" she called. "Jump onto my back!"

The sugar glider took a deep breath. Then, with all the strength he could muster, he leaped from his lily pad. But instead of gliding out toward the fox—

Whoosh!

—he catapulted up in the sky.

The bugs had formed a rope, wrapped around his ankles, and swept him up and away. Now they were zooming and darting and whipping him through the air.

"Put me down!" Bismark shrieked. "Let me gooooo!"

167

But the bugs continued to flip, flop, and fling him every which way.

"Bismark!" called Dawn. The fox kicked as hard as she could in the water, propelling her body upward. Then, with a mighty grunt, she reached high and swiped with her paw, hoping to break the bugs' rope. But she could not reach the insects.

Hee, hee, hee!

The bugs let out shrill little laughs as they grabbed Bismark by his flaps and carried him far from the fox. Then they held him high over the pool.

Bismark laughed back. "Finally!" he cried out. "Laugh all you want, little buggies! This time, the joke's on you! I have the advantage now that I'm airborne." He grinned. "You have no idea what you just got yourselves into!"

Gliding through the air with the help of the bugs, Bismark punched, kicked, and flapped at the insects swarming around him. He and the insect army fought so fiercely that they were soon spiraling together—down, down, down into the pool.

The bugs were the first to realize where they were headed and flew off. Bismark twisted in the air, still unaware of the water below. "That's right—run you cowards!" he shouted. "Run for your puny, buggy lives!"

Splash!

Before Bismark realized where he was, he plunged beneath the water's surface, whirling, twirling, and sputtering for his life. Grabbing a nearby lily pad, the sugar glider heaved and spit out a high stream of water. Then, with all of his strength, he managed to boost himself onto the floating plant. *"Mon dieu!"* he gasped. "Every time I dry off, it's right back into this infernal pool!"

Bismark keeled over, resting his hands on his knees, struggling to catch his breath. But his moment of recovery didn't last. The bugs were back, hovering in a cloud above him, ready to strike again.

The sugar glider was tired and worn out from his fight with the bugs. There was no way he could defend himself again.

Dawn was already paddling toward him, but she still had a distance to go.

"Bismark!" she called. "Hold... on...."

"Hurry, *mon amour!*" Bismark yelped. The bugs were buzzing in circles now over his tiny, bald head. Faster and faster they went, in tighter and tighter

169

loops. And then—*zoom!*—they plummeted down and resumed their vicious attack.

"Stop! Be gone! Get away!" Bismark shouted. The sugar glider swatted the air with his flaps, hoping to ward off the insects, but it was no use. He was completely outnumbered.

The sugar glider searched the water around his lily pad, hoping to find some sort of weapon—some reeds, a branch, a big leaf—anything that might help him fight. But the only thing around him was water.

Water. That's all I have, Bismark realized. *So that's what I'll have to use.* Nervously, the sugar glider leaned over the edge of the lily pad. Then he dipped his flaps in the pool and frantically started to splash.

"*Cinco, quatre,* three, *dos....*" With his eyes squeezed shut with dread, Bismark began to count down the last seconds of his life. But not a single bug attacked.

Slowly, he opened one eye, then the other. The insects were flying away! "*Quoi?* What's going on?" he wondered, allowing his flaps to rest. But as soon as he did, the bugs changed course and darted toward him once more.

"Bismark, keep splashing!" Dawn shouted, nearly there now. She gazed up at the sky. The insect army still buzzed over her head, but they were keeping their distance. Dawn flicked water up high with her paw, sending the swarm even farther away.

"Tobin, jump in!" she yelled. "You'll be safe in the water."

This was it—this was the key to this fight. This was how they'd stay safe. The fox splashed again, and as the bugs retreated even more, she gave a satisfied grin. "These bugs can't swim!"

Chapter Twenty-Two
FOX GOT YOUR TONGUE?

"Tobin, quickly!" yelled Dawn. Why wasn't the pangolin coming? He had to get in the water if he was going to be safe from the bugs.

"Oh, Dawnth, I can'th maketh over there!"

The fox peered through the insects at the shore—and saw the reason for Tobin's delay. Tobin couldn't get in the water—he was tongue-tied with King Kami! Tobin's pink tongue was on the right, Kami's purple one was on the left…and a big, terrible tangle was in the middle.

The fox opened her mouth to speak, but she was not sure what to say. Even Bismark gaped in unusual silence as he watched Tobin and King Kami twist, turn, and pull their tongues in battle.

"Ha, ha, ha!" King Kami let out a cackle. Then, curling his tail around a tree for support, the chameleon

173

gave a giant yank, jolting the pangolin forward. But after just a short stumble, Tobin dug his sharp claws in the ground. Then he returned the attack, rolling his tongue in big, vibrating waves, hoping to throw King Kami off balance. But the chameleon grabbed hold of his own tongue before the waves reached him. Then he whipped it as hard as he could. In an instant, the waves Tobin created reversed themselves, traveling back toward the pangolin and bouncing him onto his bottom.

"*Mon dieu!*" Bismark cried, hopping up and down on his lily pad. "It's a tongue-of-war!"

Breathless, Tobin scrambled back to his feet. Then, planting his heels in the ground, he jerked back a long section of his tongue, which pulled King Kami closer to him. But the chameleon quickly steadied himself, bracing his front limbs against a log.

For a moment, the two animals stood still, tongues tied, gazes locked.

"*Blingphlumplmph!*" King Kami shouted.

"*Flubnzminph!*" Tobin yelled back.

Slowly, the chameleon began to move, stepping sideways. Tobin did the same. The animals kept going, side-stepping faster and faster, until they spun at full speed in a circle, whirling around their knotted tongues.

As he went round and round, Tobin's cheeks flapped in the wind, and his dry eyes started to sting. The world was a blur of trees and grass, and bugs flew into his open mouth. The pangolin winced. With his tongue out and knotted, he couldn't swallow or spit out the insects. So the bugs remained—biting, stinging, and scratching the tender flesh inside his cheeks.

"*Mon dieu!*" Bismark shouted. "Our scaly chum is swelling like a swine!"

Dawn looked frantically at Tobin. He needed help, fast. "Bismark!" she shouted. "Stay here—you'll

be safe on the lily pad." The fox swam full-speed toward Tobin. "Just keep splashing!" she yelled, calling back over her shoulder.

"Wait, what?" Bismark yelped. He began to jump up and down in a panic. "Don't leave me, my love! Come back!" Then the sugar glider gazed down and his eyes bulged in horror. His frantic jumping had pierced a hole in his lily pad. He was sinking! *"Dios mio!"* he cried. The water was already up to his flaps. "I'm going under… again!"

But Dawn didn't hear him. Her eyes were glued to Tobin. He was dizzy, tripping over his feet, and his eyes were rolling back in his head. It was clear that he was going to lose this fight.

Dawn charged from the pool, racing to help him. With a powerful leap, she reached the top of the bank. Then, without pause, she rushed directly at the chameleon.

Gritting her teeth, the fox lifted her paw high overhead. Her claws gleamed in the moonlight as she brought them down. Then, with expert precision, she struck—piercing her nail right into the chameleon's fleshy tongue.

With an earsplitting yelp, King Kami fell to the ground and the tip of his tongue went slack, releasing his hold on the pangolin.

Suddenly free, Tobin reeled his tongue into his mouth and curled into his armored ball. Then he began to roll downhill, heading straight for the pool.

Plunk!

With a heavy splash, the pangolin landed in the glimmering water. His body, though bulky, quickly floated to the surface, and he expertly swam toward the sugar glider.

"Gracias,"—cough—*"mon   ami!"* Bismark sputtered, as he climbed up on Tobin's scales and collapsed. *"Mon dieu!"* he gasped, catching his breath as the pangolin paddled. "You sure don't look like a swimmer," he said to Tobin. "I mean, you're not exactly...trim. But I must say, you've outdone yourself, aquatic *amigo.* Truly. Look at you go!"

Tobin sighed with relief. His bug bites were soothed in the water, and Bismark was saved. Then he remembered—Dawn! Frantically, he turned toward the shore. The fox was still in a battle with King Kami. Though her claw was hooked deep in his tongue, the chameleon kept fighting, kicking his legs and thrashing his long, pointed tail.

"We have to go help her!" cried Tobin, and started to swim toward the shore.

"Let me go, Fox!" hissed the chameleon. "Or I will order my army to sting you to death!"

Dawn just pressed her claw harder. "Do your worst," she growled.

"As you wish, Fox." The chameleon cackled. Then, with a single flick of his claw, he summoned his insect army.

All at once, the bugs zoomed in and attacked, biting and stinging Dawn's skin. But the fox would not give up. She dug her claw deeper into the chameleon's tongue. King Kami shrieked in pain.

Bismark leaped up on his feet, balancing on Tobin's scales. "Get him, my powerful *princessa!*" he cheered. "Clobber that King Kami coward!"

With her claw still hooked in King Kami's tongue, she dragged the chameleon behind her toward the pool.

Bismark hopped up and down with excitement then punched his fist in the air. "Drown that evil enchanter!" he yapped. "Let's see how *he* likes a watery grave!"

But the fox shook her head no. She had something better in mind.

Chapter Twenty-Three
THE GREAT UNVEILING

"Don't even think of escape, you crazy chameleon," Bismark scowled. "You're our prisoner now, you color-shifting wizard of war, you insect enchanter, you monstrous magician!"

The sugar glider glared at the chameleon, whose tongue was still pinned by Dawn's claw.

The insect army still swarmed around Dawn, stinging and biting her, but she held onto the chameleon. The fox leaned toward him, bearing her gleaming fangs. "I won't let you go," she growled. "Not unless you order an end to this attack—now!"

The chameleon let out a tired squeal. He gazed at his tongue, with the fox's claw planted firmly in it, and he knew he was defeated.

Slowly, he lifted a trembling hand and pointed at the swarm of insects. With a swoop of his arm and a flick of his wrist, he motioned for them to cease. Immediately, the bugs stopped and fluttered softly to the ground.

Dawn removed her claw from his tongue and the chameleon reeled it back into his mouth.

"No, *mon amour!* Don't let him go!" Bismark shrieked, as he and Tobin clambered up the pool's banks. "He'll try to eat us!"

A small chuckle escaped King Kami's lips. "No, I won't. I may be a chameleon, but I'm different than most of my kind."

"Why?" asked Bismark. "Because you enjoy feasting on sugar gliders!?"

King Kami rolled one of his eyes. "Most chameleons eat bugs. But I only eat plants. That's why I can have an insect army." He grinned. "I'm a lifelong vegetarian."

Bismark placed his hands on his hips. "Well... that's fine talk, you phony, you faker, you *sham*-eleon," he ranted. "You might respect your little army here enough not to eat them, but where's your respect for our valley, hmm? Why are you stealing our life-giving water and keeping it all for yourselves...*in a drought?*"

Dawn narrowed her amber eyes. "Yes, explain."

"We were taking away what you needed most," said the chameleon, his face burning red with anger.

"But...but why?" stammered Tobin.

King Kami's eyes flickered gold. "We needed to be seen!" he bellowed.

Dawn, Bismark, and Tobin stood in stunned silence.

"You...you don't understand," said the reptile, the fight in him slipping away. "You'd *never* understand!"

"Help us to," urged the fox.

King Kami thought for a moment. Then he took a deep breath, and his face gradually softened to violet. "What do I have in common with all the insects you see here?"

"You're extremely annoying?" Bismark offered.

"You're trying to steal all the water?" Tobin guessed.

"You can all hide yourselves," pronounced Dawn. "All the creatures in the insect army are able to camouflage themselves to blend in with their background—and so can you."

"Yes," King Kami said. "We share the ability to hide ourselves in plain sight. Our enemies can't see us. We don't get eaten by our predators. But...it's not all good." One of the chameleon's eyes gazed at the moon; the other looked down at his feet. "No one notices us— no one at all!" he explained. "Just the past couple nights, we've tried so many times!"

"What do you mean?" Tobin asked.

The chameleon started to pace back and forth in front of the baffled Brigade. "You kicked us, and we screamed," he said. "No one noticed. You sat on us, and we shrieked. No one paid attention. We brought down one of your dens. You ignored us." King Kami pivoted toward his audience. "Just imagine—never being acknowledged! *Never!* Even when you try your hardest."

The Brigade gaped at the reptile. His scales were a wash of blues, his

182

hands were shaking, and his eyes were glassy.

"So...we attacked," explained the chameleon, struggling to keep his voice level. "We took control of the forest and we stole your water. We took away what you needed so *finally* you would notice us."

Tobin's eyes widened in fascination. "So the swirling sand, the tree bark, the tumbleweed—those were all your insect army?"

King Kami nodded. "They're an incredible bunch," he said. "Especially my oldest friends—the stick bugs. They're not only masters of camouflage, but masters of movement, too. They can actually mimic plants swaying in the breeze." He paused. "But you don't see any of this," he said softly. "None of it at all."

"That's right!" A shrill voice rose from the crowd, and Bismark's former walking stick scuttled in front of the sugar glider. "You didn't even notice I was alive—and you were holding me right in your hand!" he yelled.

"*Mais oui...* but how can you blame me for that?" Bismark asked, giving an innocent shrug. "You look just like...like..."

"A stick! I know!" the insect exclaimed. "But I'm a stick bug, not a stick." The nub on the end of his body turned left and right as the animal shook its head in dismay. "I was with you this entire time, planning the attacks on you. But even when I screamed out—when I yelled to my friends—you didn't notice me."

"The high-pitched shrieks!" Tobin exclaimed. He looked at Bismark. "I told you that it wasn't—"

"—it wasn't your stinker, I know," finished Bismark. "Sorry, *muchacho.*" The sugar glider grinned at his friend.

The stick bug sighed. "See? Even though you heard me, you ignored me." The stick bug turned his long body sideways then shook one of his rear limbs. "Even when you broke a piece of me off and I grew it back, you thought I was just a twig," he continued. "A stick can't regrow limbs—but a stick bug can."

Tobin twitched at a sudden wiggle on his right shoulder. The pangolin craned his neck and looked down at it. "Oh...oh goodness!" he uttered. One of his scales was moving! The pangolin and his friends gaped as it sprouted a pair of wings. It wasn't a scale after all—it was a moth!

"You never noticed me either!" it cried, fluttering and flying away.

"*Mon dieu! I knew* it!" Bismark declared. "How could I ever doubt my supreme sanity? I thought I was going crazy—but your scales were popping off after all!"

The fox lowered her head toward King Kami. "So you're responsible for all the 'evil magic' we've been experiencing," she confirmed. "You're the one who directed it."

The chameleon nodded.

Dawn shook her head. "All this violence…all this pain that you've caused…" she began.

"It's the only way you would notice us," interrupted the stick bug. "You ignored us before. We're always ignored." The group of insects behind him fluttered in agreement. "We try to speak up, but no one listens. You always think our voices are something else— the howl of the wind, the patter of rain, the rustling of leaves…the poof of a pangolin!"

Bismark gave an innocent shrug of his shoulders.

The stick bug sighed. "We just can't get noticed!"

"Oh goodness," Tobin stammered, "but we would never ignore you on purpose! We just couldn't see you."

The fox nodded. "That's right—we couldn't see

through your camouflage." She turned to the crowd. "If you want to be recognized, you have to show us you're there—but not the way you did," she chided. "You caused great harm to other creatures."

"Our friend Cora," whispered the pangolin, "she's so thirsty she can't even move! And other animals at the dry watering hole are sick because of you. Some even died!" Tobin felt a lump in his throat and a heavy weight in his stomach. Unable to hide his grief, his body trembled and he lowered his snout toward the ground.

"I'm...I'm sorry," the chameleon stammered softly. "I just—I didn't know what else to do! No one sees us...no one cares. We're...we're nobodies!" He started to wail.

Dawn, Bismark, and Tobin looked sadly at the blubbering chameleon.

"My real name isn't even King Kami!" he cried, throwing his arms up in defeat. "It's...it's..."—he paused and took a deep breath—"it's Carl!" The chameleon closed his eyes, then bowed his now deep-blue head in shame.

For a moment, the Brigade was silent. Then Dawn drew close to the reptile. "You deserve to be noticed," she said. "Everyone does."

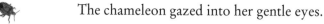

The chameleon gazed into her gentle eyes.

"But you must get noticed by doing *good,*" she stressed, "not by hurting others."

Carl nodded. "But how?" he asked.

Dawn looked toward the pool and smiled. "I can think of a great way to start."

Chapter Twenty-Four
WATER, WATER, EVERYWHERE!

Tobin awoke to the sound of footsteps and rustling leaves. "Oh—oh goodness!" he cried. He quickly uncurled, stretched his limbs, and headed toward the seasonal pool.

The previous night, in an effort to share news of the water, the Brigade had sought out the lyrebirds. Then, loudly and clearly, they stated their message, indicating the pool's location and inviting everyone to it.

While Dawn, Tobin, and Bismark set out to retrieve Cora, the lyrebirds flew off as well, mimicking the Brigade's words...and spreading them throughout the whole forest.

The pangolin was eager to see if their plan had worked. He picked up his pace and sprinted toward the pool. Had their words reached everyone in need? Had all the animals come?

When Tobin arrived at the reeds by the banks, he skidded to a stop. Anxiously, he poked his long snout through the grass. Then he gasped.

The scene was more brilliant than ever. The water was shimmering with violet, deep pinks, and green—and it was completely surrounded by animals.

Wallabies and rabbits, bilbies and bandicoots—mammals of all kinds—drank and bathed in the pool. Hawks and falcons soared in the sky then swooped down into the water. The platypus splashed with his strange, webbed feet; the armadillo splashed back with his scaly tail. Tobin smiled as he took in the crowd—happily drinking, bathing, and floating.

Then he saw Cora, and his face lit up even brighter than the glowing water before him.

"Cora!" called Tobin.

The wombat turned. "Tobin!" she cried. She ran toward the pangolin, and they hugged in a long embrace.

Tobin could still feel Cora's ribs through her fur. But after drinking and resting all day, her smile had brightened and the glimmer had returned to her eyes. It would take moons for her to heal fully, but the wombat was already getting back to her healthy and cheerful self.

Cora nuzzled against Tobin's side. "Your scales—they're not dry anymore!" she exclaimed. "They're almost as soft as my fur."

The pangolin blushed. "Nothing's as soft as your fur, Cora," he whispered.

"Well, well, well—what a heartwarming sight!" Bismark sauntered up behind Tobin and Cora then squeezed into the space between them. "Dawn, my *bella*, my sweet!" he called. "What do you say? Shall we make this a double date?" Bismark beckoned to the fox with his flap.

Dawn gave a small grin. Then, after one last sip from the pool, she walked up the bank to her friends.

"*Perfecto,*" Bismark said with a sigh. "Everything is back as it should be—thanks to the Nocturnal Brigade!" The sugar glider puffed out his chest with pride. "What a team we make, *mais oui, mon amour?*" He tossed his cape over one shoulder and gazed into Dawn's amber eyes.

"HOLD IT RIGHT THERE! NOW DIP IT!"

A booming voice cut through the clearing. A chute moved in the air. Then, obeying the voice's

191

commands, it came to a halt, lowered, and dipped down into the pool, filling with water. Then it rose again.

"AND TIP IT!"

Slowly, the chute tipped, spilling its water into another chute that hovered in the air.

Carl, perched on a rock, smiled proudly at the Brigade. With the help of the veiled creatures and their chutes, the chameleon was directing water from the pool back to the watering hole and to other places throughout the valley.

"HOLD IT RIGHT THERE! NOW TIP IT!"

As Carl repeated the familiar commands, directing the next chute in line, Dawn, Tobin, and Bismark all returned the chameleon's grin. This time, his

actions were not harming anyone—they were helping everyone.

The fox looked at the work with approval. "With Carl and the rest of the veiled creatures' help, the entire valley will have water," she said. "We'll have enough to end this drought for good."

"And to fuel my fountain of honor forever!" Bismark added.

Cora giggled and nuzzled next to her friend. Tobin beamed.

"Well," said the sugar glider, hopping in front of the group, "I'm glad everyone's happy now. I must admit—I can't imagine what it must be like to always be hidden. After all, it's impossible not to notice me. I'm a fantastic flapping phenomenon!"

"I'm a fantastic flapping phenomenon!" echoed a lyre.

Bismark frowned and wagged his finger at the pesky bird. "No, *muchacho*—there's only *one* of those— and it's me!"

"There's only one of those—and it's me!"

"It's me!"

"It's me!"

All the lyrebirds chimed in a chorus.

Bismark threw up his flaps and stomped his feet

in frustration. "No, you don't understand—it's me, *moi*, Bismark!" Suddenly, his big eyes bulged even larger—he had an idea. Standing as tall as he could, the sugar glider puffed out his chest, and cleared his throat. "*Bismark* is the boldest, bravest, and handsomest marsupial there ever was. *BISMARK!*"

The sugar glider waited eagerly for the lyrebird echo. When it came, it rang out louder than ever.

"Boldest!"

"Bravest!"

"Handsomest!"

194

"Bismark!"

"Bismark!

"BISMARK!"

The sugar glider beamed, delighted with his success. Then he happily pranced off, dancing along to the chant, with Dawn, Tobin, and Cora laughing together behind him.

Read All Four
Nocturnal Adventures!

Visit nocturnalsworld.com
to watch animated videos, download fun nighttime
activities and check out a map of the Brigade's
adventure at nocturnalsworld.com/map/

*

Teachers and Librarians get Common Core Language
Arts and Next Generation Science guides for the
book series.

*

#NocturnalsWorld

www.fabledfilms.com

About the Author

Tracey Hecht is a writer and entrepreneur who has written, directed and produced for film. She has created a Nocturnals Read Aloud Writing program for middle graders in partnership with the New York Public Library that has expanded nationwide. She splits her time between Oquossoc, Maine and New York City.

Sarah Fieber pursued her lifelong passion for writing at Yale, and has her Masters of Professional Writing from USC, and an MFA from NYU. She has published several short stories and is currently working on a new middle grade series. She lives in New York City with her dog Beau. This is her first children's book.

About the Illustrator

Kate Liebman is an artist who lives and works in New York City. She graduated from Yale University, contributes to the Brooklyn Rail, and has shown her work at various galleries.

About Fabled Films

Fabled Films is a publishing and entertainment company creating original content for middle grade and Y/A audiences. Fabled Films Press combines strong literary properties with high quality production values to connect books with generations of parents and their children. Each property is supported with additional content in the form of animated web series and social media as well as websites featuring activities for children, parents, bookstores, educators and librarians.

FABLED FILMS PRESS
NEW YORK CITY